An introduction by Rolf Harris

This is a good book in two ways – because it is full of wonderful stories, and because all the profits from the money you paid for it will be sent to The Save the Children Fund, to help children in need all over the world.

Puffins asked some of your favourite authors and artists to write or illustrate stories about something nice or surprising which happened to ordinary children and, best of all, all these writers and artists gave their work free.

So as you read these marvellous stories, you can be pleased to know that your money will be helping many other children whose stories would not make such happy reading.

Two thirds of the world's children go to bed hungry every night and The Save the Children Fund can help only a comparatively small proportion of them. But whatever you can do to assist the Fund's work either as an individual or in concert with your friends will save lives and restore happiness to children who cannot themselves say 'Thank you'. Will you let me say it on their behalf?

The Friday Miracle
and other stories

EDITED BY KAYE WEBB

BY

JOAN AIKEN   ALAN GARNER
NORMAN HUNTER   PHILIPPA PEARCE
BARBARA LEONIE PICARD
BARBARA SOFTLY   NOEL STREATFEILD
JOHN ROWE TOWNSEND   JENIFER WAYNE
URSULA MORAY WILLIAMS

with illustrations by
George Adamson   Victor Ambrus
Shirley Hughes   Charles Keeping
Richard Kennedy   Barbara Nunan
Margaret Palmer   Lalla Ward
and Fritz Wegner

published in aid of The Save the Children Fund
PENGUIN BOOKS

Penguin Books Ltd, Harmondsworth, Middlesex, England
Penguin Books Inc., 7110 Ambassador Road, Baltimore, Md 21207, U.S.A.
Penguin Books Australia Ltd, Ringwood, Victoria, Australia

—

First published 1969
Copyright © Penguin Books Ltd, 1969

*

Made and printed in Great Britain
by Hazell Watson & Viney Ltd,
Aylesbury, Bucks
Set in Linotype Juliana

CONTENTS

JOAN AIKEN

The Dark Streets of Kimball's Green

'Em! You, Em! Where has that dratted child got to? Em!
Wait till I lay hold of you, I won't half tan you!'

Mrs Bella Vaughan looked furiously up and down the short
street. She was a stocky woman, with short, thick, straight
grey hair, parted on one side and clamped back by a grip; a
cigarette always dangled from one corner of her mouth and,
as soon as it dwindled down, another grew there. 'Em!
Where have you got to?' she yelled again.

'Here I am, Mrs Vaughan!' Emmeline dashed anxiously
round the corner.

'Took long enough about it! The Welfare Lady's here,
wants to know how you're getting on. Here, let's tidy you up.'

Mrs Vaughan pulled a comb and handkerchief out of her

tight-stretched apron pocket, dragged the comb sharply through Emmeline's hair, damped the handkerchief with spit and scrubbed it over Emmeline's flinching face.

'Hullo, Emmeline. Been out playing?' said the Welfare Lady, indoors. 'That's right. Fresh air's the best thing for them, isn't it, Mrs Vaughan?'

'She's always out,' grunted Mrs Vaughan. 'Morning, noon and night. I don't hold with kids frowsting about indoors. Not much traffic round here.'

'Well, Emmeline, how are you getting on? Settling down with Mrs Vaughan, quite happy, are you?'

Emmeline looked at her feet and muttered something. She was thin and small for her age, dark-haired and pale-cheeked.

'She's a mopey kid,' Mrs Vaughan pronounced. 'Always want to be reading, if I didn't tell her to run out of doors.'

'Fond of reading, are you?' the Welfare Lady said kindly. 'And what do you read, then?'

'Books,' muttered Emmeline. The Welfare Lady's glance strayed to the huge, untidy pile of magazines on the telly.

'Kid'll read anything she could lay hands on, if I let her,' Mrs Vaughan said. 'I don't though. What good does reading do you? None that I know of.'

'Well, I'm glad you're getting on all right, Emmeline. Be a good girl and do what Mrs Vaughan tells you. And I'll see you next month again.' She got into her tiny car and drove off to the next of her endless list of calls.

'Right,' said Mrs Vaughan. 'I'm off too, down to the town hall to play bingo. So you hop it, and mind you're here on the doorstep at eleven sharp or I'll skin you.'

Emmeline murmured something.

'Stay indoors? Not on your nelly! And have them saying, if the house burnt down, that I oughtn't to have left you on your own?'

'It's so cold out.' A chilly September wind scuffled the bits of paper in the street. Emmeline shivered in her thin coat.

'Well, run about then, and keep warm! Fresh air's good for you, like that interfering old busybody said. Anyway she's come and gone for the month, that's something. Go on, hop it now.'

So Emmeline hopped it.

*

Kimball's Green, where Mrs Vaughan had her home, was a curious, desolate little corner of London. It lay round the top of a hill, which was crowned with a crumbling, blackened church, St Chad's. The four or five streets of tiny, aged houses were also crumbling and blackened, all due for demolition, and most of them empty. The houses were so old that they seemed shrunk and wrinkled, like old apples or old faces, and they were immeasurably, unbelievably dirty, with the dirt of hundreds of years. Around the little hill was a flat, desolate tract of land, Wansea Marshes, which nobody had even tried to use until the nineteenth century; then it became covered with railway goods yards and brick-works and gas-works and an electric power station, all of which belched their black smoke over the little island of Kimball's Green.

*

You would hardly think anybody would choose to live in such a cut-off part; but Mrs Vaughan had been born in Sylvan Street, near the top of the hill, and she declared she wasn't going to shift until they came after her with a bulldozer. She took in foster children when they grew too old for the Wansea Orphanage, and, though it wasn't a very healthy neighbourhood, what with the smoke and the damp from the marshes, there were so many orphans, and so few homes for them to go to, that Emmeline was the latest of a large number who had stayed with Mrs Vaughan. But there were very few other children in the district now; very few inhabitants at all, except old and queer ones who camped secretly in the con-

demned houses. Most people found it too far to go to the
shops: an eightpenny bus-ride, all the way past the goods
yards and the gas-works, to Wansea High Street.

So far as anyone knew, Emmeline belonged in the neighbourhood; she had been found on the step of St Chad's one
windy March night; but in spite of this, or because of it, she
was rather frightened by the nest of little dark empty streets.
She was frightened by many things, among which were Mrs
Vaughan and her son Colin. And she particularly hated the
nights, five out of seven, when Mrs Vaughan went off to play
bingo, leaving Emmeline outside in the street. Indeed, if it
hadn't been for two friends, Emmeline really didn't know
how she could have borne those evenings.

As Mrs Vaughan's clumping steps died away down the
hill, one of the friends appeared: his thin form twined out
from between some old black railings and he rubbed encouragingly against Emmeline's ankles, sticking up his tail in
welcome.

'Oh, Scrawny! There you are,' she said with relief. 'Here,
I've saved you a piece of cheese-rind from tea.'

Old Scrawny was a tattered, battered tabby, with ragged
whiskers, crumpled ears, and much fur missing from his tail;
he had no owner and lived on what he could find; he ate the
cheese-rind with a lot of loud, vulgar, guzzling noise, and
hardly washed at all afterwards; but Emmeline loved him
dearly, and he loved her back. Every night she left her window
open and old Scrawny climbed in, by various gutters, drain-
pipes, and the wash-house roof. Mrs Vaughan wouldn't have
allowed such a thing for a minute if she had known, but
Emmeline always took care that old Scrawny had left long
before she was called in the morning.

When the rind was finished Scrawny jumped into Emmeline's arms and she tucked her hands for warmth under his
scanty fur; they went up to the end of the street by the

church, where there was a telephone booth. Like the houses around, it was old and dirty, and it had been out of order for so many years that now nobody even bothered to thump its box for coins. The only person who used it was Emmeline, and she used it almost every night, unless gangs were roaming the streets and throwing stones, in which case she hid behind a dustbin or under a flight of area steps. But when the gangs had gone elsewhere the call-box made a very convenient shelter; best of all, it was even light enough to read there, because although the bulb in the call-box had been broken long ago, a street lamp shone right overhead.

'No book tonight, Scrawny, unless Mr Yakkymo comes and brings me another,' said Emmeline, 'so what shall we do? Shall we phone somebody, or shall I tell you a story?'

Scrawny purred, dangling round her neck like a striped scarf.

'We'll ring somebody up, shall we? All right.'

She let the heavy door close behind her. Inside it was not exactly warm, but at least they were out of the wind. Scrawny climbed from Emmeline's shoulder into the compartment where the telephone books would have been if somebody hadn't made off with them; Emmeline picked up the broken receiver and dialled.

'Hullo, can I speak to King Cunobel? Hullo, King Cunobel, I am calling to warn you. A great army is approaching your fort – the Tribe of the Children of Darkness. Under their wicked queen Belavaun they are coming to attack your stronghold with spears and chariots. You must tell your men to be extra brave; each man must arm himself with his bow and a sheaf of arrows, two spears and a sword. Each man must have his faithful wolfhound by his side.' She stroked old Scrawny, who seemed to be listening intently. 'Your men are far outnumbered by the Children of Dark, King Cunobel, so you must tell your Chief Druid to prepare a magic drink, made from vetch and mallow and succory, to give them courage. The leaves must be steeped in mead and left to gather dew for two nights, until you have enough to wet each man's tongue. Then they will be brave enough to beat off the Children of Dark and save your camp.'

She listened for a moment or two with her ear pressed against the silent receiver, and then said to old Scrawny:

'King Cunobel wants to know what will happen if the Children of Dark get to the fort before the magic drink is prepared?'

'Morow,' said Scrawny. He jumped down from the bookshelf and settled himself on Emmeline's feet, where there was more room to stretch out.

'My faithful wolfhound says you must order your men to make high barricades of brambles and thorns,' Emmeline told King Cunobel. 'Build them in three rings round the encampment, and place one-third of your men inside each ring. King Cunobel and the Druids will be in the middle ring. Then each party must fight to the death in order to delay the Children of Dark until the magic drink is ready. Do you understand? Then good-bye and good luck.'

She listened again.

'He wants to know who I am,' she told Scrawny, and she said into the telephone, 'I am a friend, the Lady Emmeline, advised by her faithful enchanted wolfhound Catuscraun. I wish you well.'

Then she rang off and said to Scrawny, 'Do you think I had better call the Chief Druid and tell him to hurry up with that magic drink?'

Old Scrawny shut his eyes.

'No,' she agreed, 'you're right, it would only distract him. I know, I'll ring up the wicked Queen of Dark.'

She dialled again and said:

'Hullo, is that the wicked Queen Belavaun? This is your

greatest enemy, ringing up to tell you that you will never, never capture the stronghold of King Cunobel. Not if you besiege it for three thousand years! King Cunobel has a strong magic that will defeat you. All your tribes, the Trinovans and the Votadins and the Damnons and the Bingonii will be eaten by wolves and wild boars. Not a man will remain! And you will lose all your weath and power and your purple robes and fur cloaks, you will have nothing left but a miserable old mud cabin outside King Cunobel's stronghold, and every day his men will look over the walls and laugh at you. Good-bye, and bad luck to you forever!'

She rang off and said to Scrawny, 'That frightened her.'

Scrawny was nine-tenths asleep, but at this moment footsteps coming along the street made him open his eyes warily. Emmeline was alert, too. The call-box made a good look-out point, but it would be a dangerous place in which to be trapped.

'It's all right,' she said to Scrawny, then. 'It's only Mr Yakkymo.'

She opened the door and they went to meet their other friend.

Mr Yakkymo (he spelt his name Iachimo, but Yakkymo was the way it sounded) came limping slightly up the street until he reached them; then he rubbed the head of old Scrawny (who stuck his tail up) and handed Emmeline a book. It was old and small, with a mottled binding and gilt-edged leaves; it was called *The Ancient History of Kimball's Green and Wansea Marshes*, and it came from Wansea Borough Library.

Emmeline's eyes opened wide with delight. She began reading the book at once, skipping from page to page.

'Why, this tells all about King Cunobel! It's even better than the one you brought about ancient London. Have you read this, Mr Yakkymo?'

He nodded, smiling. He was a thin, bent old man with

rather long white hair; as well as the book he carried a leather case, which contained a flute, and when he was not speaking he would often open this case and run his fingers absently up and down the instrument.

'I thought you would find it of interest,' he said. 'It's a pity Mrs Vaughan won't let you go to the public library yourself.'

'She says reading only puts useless stuck-up notions in people's heads,' Emmeline said dreamily, her eyes darting up and down the pages of the book. 'Listen! It tells what King Cunobel wore – a short kilt with a gold belt. His chest was painted blue with woad, and he had a gold collar round his neck and a white cloak with gold embroidery. He carried a shield of beaten brass and a short sword. On his head he wore a fillet of gold, and on his arm gold armlets. His house was built of mud and stone, with a thatched roof; the walls were hung with skins and the floor strewn with rushes.'

They had turned and were walking slowly along the street; old Scrawny, after the manner of cats, sometimes loitered behind investigating doorsteps and dark crannies, sometimes darted ahead and then waited for them to come up with him.

'Do you think any of King Cunobel's descendants still live here?' Emmeline said.

'It is just possible.'

'Tell me some more about what it was like here then.'

'All the marshes – the part where the brickworks and the goods yards are now – would have been covered by forest and threaded by slow-flowing streams.'

'Threaded by slow-flowing streams,' Emmeline murmured to herself.

'All this part would be Cunobel's village. Little mud huts, each with a door and a chimney hole, thatched with reeds.'

Emmeline looked at the pavements and rows of houses, trying to imagine them away, trying to imagine forest trees and little thatched huts.

16

'There would be a stockade of logs and thorns all round. A bigger hall for the king, and one for the Druids near the sacred grove.'

'Where was that?'

'Up at the top of the hill, probably. With a specially sacred oak in the middle. There is an oak tree, still, in St Chad's churchyard; maybe it's sprung from an acorn of the Druids' oak.'

'Maybe it's the same one? Oaks live a long time, don't they?'

'Hark!' he said checking. 'What's that?'

The three of them were by the churchyard wall; they kept still and listened. Next moment they all acted independently, with the speed of long practice: Mr Iachimo, murmuring, 'Good night, my child,' slipped away round a corner; Emmeline wrapped her precious book in a polythene bag and poked it into a hole in the wall behind a loose stone; then she and old Scrawny raced downhill, back to Mrs Vaughan's house. She crouched panting on the doorstep, old Scrawny leapt up on to a shed roof and out of reach, just as a group of half a dozen people came swaggering and singing along the street.

'What was that?' one of them called.

'A cat.'

'Let's go after it!'

'No good. It's gone.'

When they got to Mrs Vaughan's their chief left the others and came over to Emmeline.

'It's you, is it, Misery?' he said. 'Where's Ma?'

'Out at bingo.'

'She would be. I wanted to get a bit of the old girl's pension off her before she spent it all.'

He gave Emmeline's hair a yank and flipped her nose, hard and painfully, with his thumbnail. She looked at him in stony silence, biting her lip.

'Who's *she*, Col?' a new gang-member asked. 'Shall we chivvy her?'

'She's one of my Ma's orphanage brats – just a little drip. Ma won't let me tease her, so long as she's indoors, or on the step. But watch it, you, if we catch you in the street.' Colin flipped Emmeline's nose again and they drifted off, kicking at anything that lay on the pavement.

At half-past eleven Mrs Vaughan came home from her bingo and let in the shivering Emmeline, who went silently up to her bed in the attic. At eleven thirty-five old Scrawny jumped with equal silence on to her stomach, and the two friends curled round each other for warmth.

*

Colin was not at breakfast next morning. Often he spent nights on end away from home; his mother never bothered to ask where.

Emmeline had to run errands and do housework in the morning but in the afternoon Mrs Vaughan, who wanted a nap, told her to clear off and not show her face a minute before six. That gave her five whole hours for reading; she dragged on her old coat and flew up to the churchyard.

The door in the high black wall was always kept locked, but somebody had once left a lot of rusty old metal pipes stacked in an angle of the wall; Emmeline, who weighed very little more than old Scrawny, clambered carefully up them, and so over.

Inside, the churchyard was completely overgrown. Blackthorn, plane and sycamore trees were entangled with great clumps of bramble. Groves of mares' tails, chin-high to Emmeline, covered every foot of the ground. It made a perfect place to come and hide by day, but was too dark at night and too full of pitfalls; pillars and stone slabs leaned every which way, hidden in the vegetation.

Admiral

Emmeline flung herself down on the flat tomb of Admiral Sir Horace Tullesley Campbell and read her book; for three hours she never moved; then she closed it with a sigh, so as to leave some for the evening in case Mrs Vaughan went out.

A woodpecker burst yammering from the tallest tree as Emmeline shut the book. Could that be the Druids' oak, she wondered, and started to push her way through to it. Brambles scratched her face and tore her clothes; Mrs Vaughan would punish her but that couldn't be helped. And at last she was there. The tree stood in a little clear space of bare leaf-mould. It was an oak, a big one, with a gnarled, massive trunk and roots like knuckles thrusting out of the ground. This made an even better secret place for reading than the Admiral's tomb, and Emmeline wished once again that it wasn't too dark to read in the churchyard at night.

St Chad's big clock said a quarter to six, so she left *The Ancient History of Kimball's Green* in its plastic bag hidden in a hollow of the tree and went draggingly home; then realized, too late, that her book would be exceedingly hard to find once dark had fallen.

Mrs Vaughan, who had not yet spent all her week's money, went out to bingo again that evening, so Emmeline returned to the telephone box and rang up King Cunobel.

'Is that the King? I have to tell you that your enemies are five miles nearer. Queen Belavaun is driving a chariot with scythes on its wheels, and her wicked son Coluon leads a band of savage followers; he carries a sling and a gold-handled javelin and is more cruel than any of the band. Has the Chief Druid prepared the magic drink yet?'

She listened and old Scrawny, who as usual was sitting at her feet, said 'Prtnrow?'

'The Chief Druid says they have made the drink, Scrawny, and put it in a flagon of beaten bronze, which has been set beneath the sacred oak until it is needed. Meanwhile the warriors are feasting on wheat-cakes, boars' flesh and mead.'

Next she rang up Queen Belavaun and hissed, 'Oh wicked queen, your enemies are massing against you! You think that you will triumph, but you are wrong! Your son will be taken prisoner, and you will be turned out of your kingdom; you will be forced to take refuge with the Iceni or the Brigantes.'

It was still only half past nine, and Mr Iachimo probably would not come this evening, for two nights out of three he went to play his flute outside a theatre in the west end of London.

'Long ago I was a famous player and people came from all

over Europe to hear me,' he had told Emmeline sadly, one wet evening when they were sheltering together in the church porch.

'What happened? Why aren't you famous now?'

'I took to drink,' he said mournfully. 'Drink gives you hiccups. You can't play the flute with hiccups.'

'You don't seem to have hiccups now.'

'Now I can't afford to drink any longer.'

'So you can play the flute again,' Emmeline said triumphantly.

'True,' he agreed; he pulled out his instrument and blew a sudden dazzling shower of notes into the rainy dark. 'But now it is too late. Nobody listens; nobody remembers the name of Iachimo. And I have grown too old and tired to make them remember.'

'Poor Mr Yakkymo,' Emmeline thought, recalling this conversation. 'He could do with a drop of King Cunobel's magic drink; then he'd be able to make people listen to him.'

She craned out of the telephone box to look at St Chad's clock: quarter to ten. The streets were quiet tonight; Colin's gang had got money from somewhere and were down at the Wansea Palais.

'I'm going to get my book,' Emmeline suddenly decided. 'At least I'm going to try. There's a moon, it shouldn't be too dark to see. Coming, Scrawny?'

Scrawny intimated, stretching, that he didn't mind.

The churchyard was even stranger under the moon than by daylight; the mares'-tails threw their zebra-striped shadows everywhere and an owl flew hooting across the path; old Scrawny yakkered after it indignantly to come back and fight fair, but the owl didn't take up his challenge.

'I don't suppose it's really an owl,' Emmeline whispered. 'Probably one of Queen Belavaun's spies. We must make haste.'

Finding the oak tree was not so hard as she had feared, but finding the book was a good deal harder, because under the tree's thick leaves and massive branches no light could penetrate; Emmeline groped and fumbled among the roots until she was quite sure she must have been right round the tree at least three times. At last her right hand slipped into a deep crack; she rummaged about hopefully, her fingers closed on something, but what she pulled out was a small round object, tapered at one end. She stuck it in her coat pocket and went on searching. 'The book must be here somewhere, Scrawny; unless Queen Belavaun's spy has stolen it.'

At last she found it; tucked away where she could have sworn she had searched a dozen times already.

'Thank goodness! Now we'd better hurry, or there won't be any time for reading after all.'

Emmeline was not sorry to leave the churchyard behind; it felt *crowded*, as if King Cunobel's warriors were hiding there, shoulder to shoulder among the bushes, keeping vigilant watch; Sylvan Street outside was empty and lonely in comparison. She scurried into the phone box, clutching Scrawny against her chest.

'Now listen while I read to you about the Druids, Scrawny: they wore long white robes and they liked mistletoe – there's some mistletoe growing on that oak tree, I'm positive! – and they used rings of sacred stones, too. Maybe some of the stones in the churchyard are left over from the Druids.'

Scrawny purred agreeingly, and Emmeline looked up the hill, trying to move St Chad's church out of the way and replace it by a grove of sacred trees with aged, white-robed men among them.

Soon it was eleven o'clock: time to hide the book behind the stone and wait for Mrs Vaughan on the doorstep. Along with his mother came Colin, slouching and bad tempered.

'Your face is all scratched,' he told Emmeline. 'You look a sight.'

'What have you been up to?' Mrs Vaughan said sharply.

Emmeline was silent but Colin said, 'Reckon it's that mangy old cat she's always lugging about.'

'Don't let me see you with a cat round *this* house,' Mrs Vaughan snapped. 'Dirty, sneaking things, never know where they've been. If any cat comes in here, I tell you, I'll get Colin to wring its neck!'

Colin smiled; Emmeline's heart turned right over with horror. But she said nothing and crept off upstairs to bed; only, when Scrawny arrived later, rather wet because it had begun to rain, she clutched him convulsively tight; a few tears wouldn't make much difference to the dampness of his fur.

'Humph!' said Mrs Vaughan, arriving early and unexpectedly in Emmeline's attic. 'I thought as much!'

She leaned to slam the window but Scrawny, though startled out of sleep, could still move ten times faster than any human; he was out and over the roof in a flash.

'Look at that!' said Mrs Vaughan. 'Filthy, muddy cat's footprints all over my blankets! Well that's one job you'll do this morning, my young madam – you'll wash those blankets. And you'll have to sleep without blankets till they've dried – I'm not giving you any other. Daresay they're all full of fleas' eggs too.'

Emmeline, breakfastless, crouched over the tub in the back wash-house; she did not much mind the job, but her brain was giddy with worry about Scrawny; how could she protect him? Suppose he were to wait for her, as he sometimes did, outside the house. Mrs Vaughan had declared that she would go after him with the chopper if she set eyes on him; Colin had sworn to hunt him down.

'All right, hop it now,' Mrs Vaughan said, when the blankets satisfied her. 'Clear out, don't let me see you again before six. No dinner? Well, I can't help that, can I? You should have finished the washing by dinner-time. Oh, all right, here's a bit of bread and marge, now make yourself scarce. I can't abide kids about the house all day.'

Emmeline spent most of the afternoon in a vain hunt for Scrawny. Perhaps he had retired to some hidey-hole for a nap, as he often did at that time of day; but perhaps Colin had caught him already?

'Scrawny, Scrawny,' she called softly and despairingly at the mouths of alleys, outside gates, under trees and walls; there was no reply. She went up to the churchyard, but a needle in a hundred haystacks would be easier to find than Scrawny in that wilderness if he did not choose to wake and show himself.

Giving up for the moment Emmeline went in search of Mr Iachimo, but he was not to be found either; he had never told Emmeline where he lived and was seldom seen by daylight; she thought he probably inhabited one of the condemned houses and was ashamed of it.

It was very cold; a grey, windy afternoon turning gloomily to dusk. Emmeline pushed cold hands deep in her pockets; her fingers met and explored a round, unusual object. Then she remembered the thing she had picked up in the dark under the oak tree. She pulled it out, and found she was holding a tiny flask, made of some dark lustreless metal tarnished with age and crusted with earth. It was not quite empty; when Emmeline shook it she could hear liquid splashing about inside, but very little, not more than a few drops.

'Why,' she breathed, just for a moment forgetting her fear in the excitement of this discovery, 'it is – it *must* be the Druids' magic drink ! But why, why didn't the warriors drink it?'

She tried to get out the stopper; it was made of some hard blackish substance, wood, or leather that had become hard as wood in the course of years.

'Can I help you, my child?' said a gentle voice above her head.

Emmeline nearly jumped out of her skin – but it was only Mr Iachimo, who had hobbled silently up the street.

'Look – look, Mr Yakkymo! Look what I found under the big oak in the churchyard! It must be the Druid's magic drink – mustn't it? Made of mallow and vetch and succory, steeped in mead, to give warriors courage. It must be!'

He smiled at her; his face was very kind. 'Yes, indeed it must!' he said.

But somehow, although he was agreeing with her, for a moment Emmeline had a twinge of queer dread, as if there were nothing – nothing at all – left in the world to hold on to; as if even kind Mr Iachimo were not what he seemed but, perhaps, a spy sent by Queen Belavaun to steal the magic flagon.

Then she pushed down her fear, taking a deep breath, and said, 'Can you get the stopper out, Mr Yakkymo?'

'I can try,' he said, and brought out a tiny foreign-looking penknife shaped like a fish with which he began prising at the fossil-hard black substance in the neck of the bottle. At last it began to crumble.

'Take care – do take care,' Emmeline said. 'There's only a very little left. Perhaps the defenders did drink most of it. But anyway there's enough left for you, Mr Yakkymo.'

'For me, my child? Why for me?'

'Because you need to be made brave so that you can make people listen to you play your flute.'

'Very true,' he said thoughtfully. 'But do not you need bravery too?'

Emmeline's face clouded. 'What good would bravery do

me?' she said. 'I'm all right – it's old Scrawny I'm worried about. Oh, Mr Yakkymo, Colin and Mrs Vaughan say they are going to *kill* Scrawny. What can I do?'

'You must tell them they have no right to.'

'*That* wouldn't do any good,' Emmeline said miserably. 'Oh! – You've got it out!'

The stopper had come out, but it had also crumbled away entirely.

'Never mind,' Emmeline said. 'You can put in a bit of the cotton-wool that you use to clean your flute. What does it smell of, Mr Yakkymo?'

His face had changed as he sniffed; he looked at her oddly. 'Honey and flowers,' he said.

Emmeline sniffed too. There was a faint – very faint – aromatic, sweet fragrance.

'Wet your finger, Mr Yakkymo, and lick it! Please do! It'll help you, I know it will!'

'Shall I?'

'Yes do, do!'

He placed his finger across the opening, and quickly turned the bottle upside down and back, then looked at his finger-tip. There was the faintest drop of moisture on it.

'Quick – don't waste it,' Emmeline said, breathless with anxiety.

He licked his finger.

'Well? Does it taste?'

'No taste.' But he smiled, and bringing out a wad of cotton tissue, stuffed a piece of it into the mouth of the flask, which he handed to Emmeline.

'This is yours, my child. Guard it well! Now, as to your friend Scrawny – I will go and see Mrs Vaughan tomorrow, if you can protect him until then.'

'Thank you!' she said. 'The drink *must* be making you brave!'

Above their heads the clock of St Chad had tolled six.

'I must be off to the West End,' Mr Iachimo said. 'And you had better run home to supper. Till tomorrow, then – and a thousand, thousand thanks for your help.'

He gave her a deep, foreign bow and limped, much faster than usual, away down the hill.

'Oh, do let it work,' Emmeline thought, looking after him.

Then she ran home to Mrs Vaughan's.

Supper was over; Colin, thank goodness, did not come in, and Mrs Vaughan wanted to get through and be off; Emmeline bolted down her food, washed the plates, and was dismissed to the streets again.

As she ran up to the churchyard wall, with her fingers tight clenched round the precious little flask, a worrying thought suddenly struck her.

The magic drink had mead in it. Suppose the mead were to give Mr Iachimo hiccups? But there must be very little mead in such a tiny drop, she consoled herself; the risk could not be great.

When she pulled her book from the hole in the wall a sound met her ears that made her smile with relief: old Scrawny's mew of greeting, rather creaking and scratchy, as he dragged himself yawning, one leg at a time, from a clump of ivy on top of the wall.

'*There* you are, Scrawny! If you knew how I'd been worrying about you!'

She tucked him under one arm, put the book under the other, and made her way to the telephone box. Scrawny settled on her feet for another nap, and she opened *The Ancient History of Kimball's Green*. Only one chapter remained to be read; she turned to it and became absorbed. St Chad's clock ticked solemnly round overhead.

When Emmeline finally closed the book, tears were running down her face.

'Oh, Scrawny – they didn't win! They lost! King Cuno-bel's men were all killed – and the Druids too, defending the stronghold. Every one of them. Oh, how can I bear it? Why did it have to happen, Scrawny?'

Scrawny made no answer, but he laid his chin over her ankle. At that moment the telephone bell rang.

Emmeline stared at the instrument in utter consternation. Scrawny sprang up; the fur along his back slowly raised, and his ears flattened. The bell went on ringing.

'But,' whispered Emmeline, staring at the broken black receiver, 'it's out of order. It *can't* ring! It's never rung! What shall I do, Scrawny?'

By now, Scrawny had recovered. He sat himself down again and began to wash. Emmeline looked up and down the empty street. Nobody came. The bell went on ringing.

At that same time, down below the hill and some distance off, in Wansea High Street, ambulance attendants were care-fully lifting an old man off the pavement and laying him on a stretcher.

'Young brutes,' said a bystander to a policeman who was taking notes. 'It was one of those gangs of young hooligans from up Kimball's Green way; I'd know several of them again if I saw them. They set on him – it's the old street musician who comes up from there too. Seems he was coming home early tonight, and the boys jumped on him – you wouldn't think they'd bother with a poor fellow like him, he can't have much worth stealing.'

But the ambulance men were gathering up handfuls of half-crowns and two-shilling pieces which had rolled from Mr Iachimo's pockets; there were notes as well, ten shillings, a pound, even five- and ten-pound notes. And a broken flute.

'It was certainly worth their while tonight,' the policeman said. 'He must have done a lot better than usual.'

'He was a game old boy – fought back like a lion; marked some of them, I shouldn't wonder. They had to leave him and run for it. Will he be all right?'

'We'll see,' said the ambulance man, closing the doors.

'I'd better answer it,' Emmeline said at last. She picked up the receiver, trembling as if it might give her a shock.

'Hullo?' she whispered.

And a voice – a faint, hoarse, distant voice – said,

'This is King Cunobel. I cannot speak for long. I am calling to warn you. There is danger on the way – great danger coming towards you and your friend. Take care! Watch well!'

Emmeline's lips parted. She could not speak.

'There is danger – danger!' the voice repeated. Then the line went silent.

Emmeline stared from the silent telephone to the cat at her feet.

'Did you hear it too, Scrawny?'

Scrawny gazed at her impassively, and washed behind his ear.

Then Emmeline heard the sound of running feet. The warning had been real. She pushed the book into her pocket and was about to pick up Scrawny, but hesitated, with her fingers on the little flask.

'Maybe I ought to drink it, Scrawny? Better that than have it fall into the enemy's hands. Should I? Yes, I will! Here, you must have a drop too.'

She laid a wet finger on Scrawny's nose; out came his pink tongue at once. Then she drained the bottle, picked up Scrawny, opened the door, and ran.

Turning back once more to look, she could see a group of dark figures coming after her down the street. She heard someone shout,

'That's her, and she's got the cat too! Come on!'

But beyond, behind, and *through* her pursuers, Emmeline caught a glimpse of something else: a high, snow-covered hill, higher than the hill she knew, crowned with great bare trees. And on either side of her, among and in front of the dark houses, as if she were seeing two pictures, one printed on top of the other, were still more trees, and little thatched stone houses. Thin animals with red eyes slunk silently among the huts. Just a glimpse she had, of the two worlds, one behind the other, and then she had reached Mrs Vaughan's doorstep and turned to face the attackers.

Colin Vaughan was in the lead; his face, bruised, cut, and furious, showed its ugly intention as plainly as a raised club.

'Give me that damn cat. I've had enough from you and your friends. I'm going to wring its neck.'

But Emmeline stood at bay; her eyes blazed defiance and so did Scrawny's; he bared his fangs at Colin like a sabre-toothed tiger.

Emmeline said clearly, 'Don't you dare lay a finger on me, Colin Vaughan. Just don't you dare touch me!'

He actually flinched, and stepped back half a pace; his gang shuffled back behind him.

At this moment Mrs Vaughan came up the hill; not at her usual smart pace but slowly, plodding, as if she had no heart in her.

'Clear out, the lot of you,' she said angrily. 'Poor old Mr Iachimo's in the Wansea Hospital, thanks to you. Beating up old men! That's all you're good for. Go along, scram, before I set the back of my hand to some of you. Beat it!'

'But we were going to wring the cat's neck. You wanted me to do that,' Colin protested.

'Oh, what do I care about the blame cat?' she snapped, turning to climb the steps, and came face to face with Emmeline.

'Well, don't *you* stand there like a lump,' Mrs Vaughan

said angrily. 'Put the blasted animal down and get to bed!'

'I'm not going to bed,' Emmeline said. 'I'm not going to live with you any more.'

'Oh, indeed? And where are you going, then?' said Mrs Vaughan, completely astonished.

'I'm going to see poor Mr Yakkymo. And then I'm going to find someone who'll take me and Scrawny, some place where I shall be happy. I'm never coming back to your miserable house again.'

'Oh, well, suit yourself,' Mrs Vaughan grunted. 'You're not the only one. I've just heard: fifty years in this place and then fourteen days' notice to quit. In two weeks the bull-dozers are coming.'

She went indoors.

But Emmeline had not listened; clutching Scrawny, brushing past the gang as if they did not exist, she ran for the last time down the dark streets of Kimball's Green.

TWO LETTERS

(from the files of The Save the Children Fund)

FROM A SMALL KOREAN BOY
TO HIS SPONSOR IN EDINBURGH

MY thanks that you have sent the money. I am now become
a pair of trousers, two under-trousers and two warm shirts.
. . . I am very happy.

FROM A SCHOOLBOY IN
LESOTHO (AFRICA)

KIND Friends, It was to my greatest surprise when I received
some parcel present from you. My gratitude is beyond the
utmost reach of human thought and there is no words to
express. Could I tabulate the things I bought with it, you
would be shocked with pleasure.

I have bought by it these are the things: a bag for carrying my school books; books, a blazer and a full school uniform. As I fail to hit on the right verb to express my great
thanks I think all my gratitude should be expressed in four
words which I think they are not little as far as I am concerned. The great words are – 'thank you very much'.

Yours obediently,

Kingsley Salepe.

ALAN GARNER

Small World

DAI shepherd dropped his crook and cried, 'Enough
of living in Llanfairpwllgwyngyllgogerychwyrndrobwll-
llantysiliogogogoch ! I'll emigrate to a place less tough.'
New Zealand beckoned. Off he flew.

   He herds the sheep at Taumatawhakatangihangakoauauatama-
teaturipukakapikimaungahoronukupokaiwhenuakitanatahu.

NORMAN HUNTER

Peril at Pagwell College

A PROFESSOR BRANESTAWM STORY

A VERY tall, black spider, with too many legs, stood in the Science Room at Pagwell College. 'Pay careful attention,' it said, in a thin, lemon-flavoured voice, 'as I shall require you to take notes later on.'

It was Mr Stinckz-Bernagh, the science master, in his black gown that was torn into spider-leggy strips at the edges. He was taking Form 3½ in chemistry. There were five rows of assorted boys. Some were in Form 3½ because they just couldn't make Form 4; others were there because they were a bit on the smart side and used to get the answers in Form 3 before the masters did.

'Please sir,' said a fattish boy with sticking-out ears, 'will this make us into chemists, sir?'

'Certainly not,' said Mr Stinckz-Bernagh, whisking the torn ribbony ends of his black gown out of the way of a little gas flame that seemed to fancy them.

'What's it for then, sir?' asked a short pale boy in long dark trousers.

Mr Stinckz-Bernagh stuck out his jaw and moved it about as if he were chewing nougat, which he wasn't; but it made him look fierce, which he definitely was.

'Everything is composed of chemicals,' he said, as if this answered the question. 'You are all nothing more than a few packets of chemicals.' He pointed a skinny finger at the boys. Before they had time to fancy themselves as packets of *Pot. Chlor., Amm. Nit.* and *Sulph. Whatsit,* the door flew open and a rather elderly schoolboy with a nervous face came in.

'Please sir, the Headmaster wants to see you in his garden,' he said, 'Professor Branestawm sir, is there sir, please sir.'

'Ha!' cried Mr Stinckz-Bernagh. 'We shall continue this lesson later. Grizzlebut, stay here and keep order while I am away.'

He shot out, followed rapidly by the torn ends of his gown which only just escaped being shut in the door.

'Got any suckers, Grizzlebut?' asked big ears.

'Shut up,' said Grizzlebut, 'I've got to keep order. He said so.'

A long skinny boy with a lot of hair got up and went behind the desk. 'Now pay attention to the next experiment,' he said, sticking his jaw out to make himself look like Mr Stinckz-Bernagh, which it didn't. He picked up a bottle. 'We have here a substance called . . .' He looked at the label, found he couldn't pronounce it and went on. 'A substance which we pour into this . . . this back answer,' he said.

'Retort,' said big ears, 'that's a retort, that's what that is.'

'Look here, you can't do that,' protested Grizzlebut, 'you aren't allowed to mess about with the chemicals.'

Long hair tipped the contents of the bottle into a sort of long-nosed glass teapot that was sitting on a little gas ring. Back answer would have been a good name for it. It exploded with a bright-green bang and several million stars.

'Coo!' shouted the class.

A clump of the stars landed in a little bowl of dirty powder. Whee, ziziziz pop boing! Tongues of flame shot out in all directions.

'Ooer!' cried the class. Grizzlebut seized a glass of water and threw it at the flames. They threw it back in the form of very sizzly steam. Then two or three jars of very quick-tempered chemicals resented all these goings on and blew up themselves, just to show that it wasn't only retorts and dirty powders that could do it.

Bang, boom, cracketty crash! Popetty fizzle boingngngng-ng bong! The science room was full of smoke, fountains of coloured flame tore across the room. Long hair made a dash for the door, was beaten to it by half an inch by Grizzlebut, and the rest of the class fell on them. Bongetty bong, swoosh pow!

Firework displays were nothing to it. A helping of ceiling came down and a column of white hot goodness-knows-what started to build up in the middle of the floor.

The boys tugged at the door handle. But Mr Stinckz-Bernagh had locked the door to stop them dodging the rest of his lesson.

Fourteen feet of dark purple smoke descended on them.

'Help!' yelled the boys.

*

'Help!' cried the Headmaster, to Professor Branestawm, out in the garden. 'Help with the gardening is what we are most

37

in need of, er, I should say of what we are most . . . that is to say what we badly need.' He hurriedly straightened out his grammar in case anybody important was listening.

'Yes, of course, er um ah exactly,' murmured the Professor, who was the only other important person there and he hadn't been listening. He was considerably occupied trying to fasten together a machine that looked something like an inside-out lawn mower with funnels.

'Labour-saving machines are the best means of coping with shortage of labour,' said Mr Stinckz-Bernagh, putting his hands behind him, rocking backwards and forwards on his toes and nearly falling into a pond occupied by a very disagreeable-looking fish.

Professor Branestawm turned a wheel and pulled a little skinny lever. The machine stuck a small spade into a flower bed, lifted up a dollop of wet earth and put it in the Headmaster's pocket.

'Gardeners are so difficult to get,' said the Headmaster, shaking the earth out on to Mr Stinckz-Bernagh. 'They find it more, ah, paying I think the term is, to get employment at the new hygienic sausage factory.'

'Not to mention free hygienic sausages twice a week,' put in Mr Stinckz-Bernagh, flipping the wet earth over to the Professor.

'Now perhaps you will be good enough to demonstrate to us your gardening invention,' said the Headmaster.

'This is the geranium-planting-out gear,' said Professor Branestawm, putting on his demonstration spectacles. The machine dug a neat hole in the lawn and planted a feather duster, which the Professor had brought to represent a geranium, the real thing being a bit out of season.

Just then a window of the Science Room opened. It opened in fifty places at once and did it by firing all the glass out in little bits, like crystal confetti. Pretty, but alarming.

'Good gracious!' cried the Headmaster.

A sheet of flame accompanied by mixed bottles and exploding test tubes came out after the glass.

'The chemistry class!' yelled Mr Stinckz-Bernagh.

He tried to climb through the broken window but was instantly set on fire by a set of flaming thingummys and immediately extinguished by an explosion that blew his gown off.

'Dear, dear,' muttered the Professor, feeling that something had gone wrong somewhere but not seeing that it could be anything to do with his gardening machine, which was now happily digging fancy holes across the lawn.

'Branestawm, by jove what's up by gad sir!' came a shout

from the road. It was Colonel Dedshott, marching happily on his way to a grand reunion tea of old Pagwellian ex Catapult Cavaliers, mostly over ninety.

Of course the Colonel took it for granted it was the Professor's invention that had started everything; because the Professor was definitely there and so absolutely was one of his inventions. And when Professor Branestawm and one of his inventions occurred simultaneously you could usually look out for bangy stuff. Only this lot didn't need much looking out for. It was making itself plentifully noticeable without any help.

Boom! Two red-hot desks came sailing through the air and landed on the rhododendrons.

'We must save the boys,' shouted Mr Stinckz-Bernagh. 'The boys! They're locked in the Science Room.' He tore round to the front entrance of Pagwell College. Colonel Dedshott tore after him. The Headmaster tore round in circles, trying to stop the Professor's hole-digging machine and do something about saving the boys, both at once, and succeeding only in treading on a highly prickly plant which promptly stuck needles into his sitting-down part.

'Help!' yelled the Headmaster. He shot off after the Colonel and Mr Stinckz-Bernagh, calling out Latin exclamations in a very educated voice.

'Save the boys!' shouted Mr Stinckz-Bernagh.

'Save the children!' roared Colonel Dedshott, who'd read that somewhere.

'Save for the future,' advised a Pagwell Bank poster on the wall.

'Save one and tuppence,' screamed a packet of supermarket sausages in a shop opposite.

'God save the Queen,' squeaked an inferior gramophone someone had set off by mistake.

Smoke and stars, burning bottles and glowing globules

came hurtling out of the Science Room window. Chemical catastrophe howled round Professor Branestawm's head.

'I really think this er chemistry business is taken too seriously at schools nowadays,' he said, shaking his head and switching the gardening machine over to digging up the Headmaster's prize dahlias, which it did rather well.

Swish! A two gallon jar of boiling acid shot past the Professor's left ear, disarranging his five pairs of spectacles.

'Tut tut, this is most careless,' he cried, 'I really must make a complaint to the . . .' Slosh! A square yard of jelly sort of stuff flopped out of the window and a very unclean glass jar landed on the gardening machine.

That did it. No invention of Professor Branestawm's was going to stand that sort of impertinence. The machine heaved up a shovelful of earth and three Class 1 dahlias and dumped them on the jelly.

Pale-blue flame lapped out of the Science Room window.

The gardening machine slung a shovelful of earth through the window. The Science Room returned it red hot and smelling highly unpleasant.

'Dear dear, I must make some adjustment,' began the Professor. But his gardening machine had got its mad properly up and had no intention of being adjusted. It scooped up an entire bed of Gesiggieclokkie Grandiflora and slung it through the window. It followed this by half a ton of well-manured soil.

The Professor pulled the biggest lever he could see. It came off in his hand.

Twenty spadefuls of compost and a cubic yard of wet leaf mould went through the window.

Outside the Science Room door there was nearly as much energetic pandemonium as inside the room.

Mr Stinckz-Bernagh dived into his pocket for the key. His

fist went clean through the pocket and the key went clanketty clank down a grating.

Colonel Dedshott hurled himself at the door.

The boys inside screeched like a thousand parrots disagreeing with one another.

Smoke belched through cracks in the door. Flames came creeping under the door. The Colonel stamped on them and they crept back.

Out in the garden the Professor's machine threw the lawn through the window.

Floomph, phut plip wuff umph. The flames went out. The explosions stopped. The smoke very nearly cleared away.

The Headmaster with great presence of mind at last remembered his own bunch of keys, found the right one after only seven goes, and threw open the Science Room door.

The dirtiest looking scrabble of boys he had ever seen in his many years' experience of boys connected with dirt of innumerable kinds, came out.

'Please sir, we sir, help sir,' they gasped.

'I er am afraid my gardening machine has rather spoiled your garden, Headmaster,' said the Professor after some sorting out had been done. 'Some substance fell out of a window on it and dis, ah, rupted the self acting re-oscillating . . .'

'To blazes with the garden!' cried the Headmaster, which in point of fact is exactly where most of it had gone to. 'The boys are saved, that's all that matters. The place is insured. We can re-build.'

So for once one of Professor Branestawm's inventions actually saved the situation by being put wrong by an outside disaster which it then put right.

Pagwell College was closed for two weeks, for repairs. This enabled Form $3\frac{1}{2}$ to be got fairly clean again by a set of extremely energetic mums and plenty of soap and water.

A LETTER

FROM HIS HOLINESS THE DALAI LAMA

to Tibetan children in exile

CHILDREN, you are like flowers about to bloom. We will try our best to protect you and to see that you flourish. I have yet an important thing to tell you. This is to be very friendly and united among yourselves. You are all children of one race who have suffered so much together. Your present thoughts are the same and your future is one.

You must always behave yourselves wherever you are. Everything you do will be noticed. If one behaves well then all Tibetans are benefited, but if one behaves badly all the others are put to shame...

Children, our country will surely one day regain its independence and every one of us, even the animals, will be happy again. Even so, we must not just wait as if waiting for the rain to fall from the sky. We must work hard, and old and young must strive to achieve our common end.

PHILIPPA PEARCE

Return to Air

THE Ponds are very big, so that at one end people bathe and at the other end they fish. Old chaps with bald heads sit on folding stools and fish with rods and lines, and little kids squeeze through the railings and wade out into the water to fish with nets. But the water's much deeper at our end of the Ponds, and that's where we bathe. You're not allowed to bathe there unless you can swim; but I've always been able to swim. They used to say that was because fat floats – well, I don't mind. They call me Sausage.

Only, I don't dive – not from any diving-board, thank you. I have to take my glasses off to go into the water, and I can't see without them, and I'm just not going to dive, even from the lowest diving-board, and that's that, and they stopped nagging about it long ago.

Then, this summer, they were all on to me to learn duck-diving. You're swimming on the surface of the water and

45

suddenly you up-end yourself just like a duck and dive down deep into the water, and perhaps you swim about a bit under-water, and then come up again. I daresay ducks begin doing it soon after they're born. It's different for them.

So I was learning to duck-dive – to swim down to the bot-tom of the Ponds, and pick up a brick they'd throw in, and bring it up again. You practise that in case you have to rescue anyone from drowning – say, they'd sunk for the third time, and gone to the bottom. Of course, they'd be bigger and heavier than a brick, but I suppose you have to begin with bricks and work up gradually to people.

The swimming-instructor said, 'Sausage, I'm going to throw the brick in –' It was a brick with a bit of old white flannel round it, to make it show up underwater. '– Sausage, I'm going to throw it in, and you go *after* it – go *after* it, Sausage, and get it before it reaches the bottom and settles in the mud, or you'll never get it.'

He'd made everyone come out of the water to give me a chance, and they were standing watching. I could see them blurred along the bank, and I could hear them talking and laughing; but there wasn't a sound in the water except me just treading water gently, waiting. And then I saw the brick go over my head as the instructor threw it, and there was a splash as it went into the water ahead of me; and I thought: I can't do it – my legs won't up-end this time – they feel just flabby – they'll float, but they won't up-end – they *can't* up-end – it's different for ducks. . . . But while I was thinking all that, I'd taken a deep breath, and then my head really went down and my legs went up into the air – I could feel them there, just air around them, and then there was water round them, because I was going down into the water, after all. Right down into the water; straight down. . . .

At first my eyes were shut, although I didn't know I'd shut them. When I did realize, I forced my eyelids up against the

water to see. Because, although I can't see much without my glasses, as I've said, I don't believe anyone could see much underwater in those Ponds; so I could see as much as anyone.

The water was like a thick greeny-brown lemonade, with wispy little things moving very slowly about in it – or perhaps they were just movements of the water, not things at all; I couldn't tell. The brick had a few seconds' start of me, of course, but I could still see a whitish glimmer that must be the flannel round it: it was ahead of me, fading away into the lower water, as I moved after it.

The funny thing about swimming underwater is its being so still and quiet and shady down there, after all the air and sunlight and splashing and shouting just up above. I was shut right in by the quiet, greeny-brown water, just me alone with the brick ahead of me, both of us making towards the bottom.

The Ponds are deep, but I knew they weren't too deep; and, of course, I knew I'd enough air in my lungs from the breath I'd taken. I knew all that.

Down we went, and the lemonade-look quite went from the water, and it became just a dark blackish-brown, and you'd wonder you could see anything at all. Especially as the bit of white flannel seemed to have come off the brick by the time it reached the bottom and I'd caught up with it. The brick looked different down there, anyway, and it had already settled right into the mud – there was only one corner left sticking up. I dug into the mud with my fingers and got hold of the thing, and then I didn't think of anything except getting up again with it into the air.

Touching the bottom like that had stirred up the mud, so that I began to go up through a thick cloud of it. It made me feel I might be getting lost. Perhaps I'd swum underwater too far – perhaps I'd come up at the far end of the Ponds among all the fishermen and foul their lines and perhaps get a fishhook caught in the flesh of my cheek. Or perhaps I just wasn't going to find the top and the air again . . .

The funny thing was that I only began to be afraid on the way back. Even though I was going up quite quickly, and the water was already changing from brown-black to green-brown and then to bright lemonade; I could almost see the sun shining through the water, I was getting so near the surface. It wasn't until then that I felt really frightened: I knew I was moving much too slowly; I knew I would never reach the air again in time.

Never the air again . . .

Then suddenly I was at the surface — I'd exploded back from the water into the air. For a while I couldn't think of anything, and I couldn't do anything except let out the old breath I'd been holding and take a couple of fresh, quick ones, and tread water — and hang on to that brick.

Pond water was trickling down inside my nose and into my mouth, which I hate. But there was air all round and above, for me to breathe, to live; and I might live to be a hundred now, and keep a sweet-shop of my own, and walk on the Moon, and breed mastiffs, and rescue someone from drowning and be awarded a medal for it and be interviewed on TV.

And then I noticed they were shouting from the bank. They were cheering and shouting, 'Sausage! Sausage!' and the instructor was hallooing with his hands round his mouth and bellowing to me: 'What on earth have you got there, Sausage?'

So then I turned myself properly round — I'd come up almost facing the fishermen at the other end of the Ponds, but otherwise only a few feet from where I'd gone down; so that was all right. I turned round and swam to the bank and they hauled me out and gave me my glasses to have a good look at what I'd brought up from the bottom.

Because it wasn't a brick. It was just about the size and shape of one, but it was a tin – an old, old tin-box with no paint left on it and all brown-black slime from the bottom of the Ponds. It was as heavy as a brick because it was full of mud. Don't get excited, as we did: there was nothing there but mud. We strained all the mud through our fingers, but there wasn't anything else there – not even a bit of old sandwich or the remains of bait. I thought there might have been, because the tin could have belonged to one of the old chaps

that have always fished at the other end of the Ponds. They often bring their dinners with them in bags or tins, and they have tins for bait, too. It could have been dropped into the water at their end of the Ponds and got moved to our end with the movement of the water. Otherwise I don't know how that tin can have got there. Anyway, it must have been there for years and years, by the look of it. When you think, it might have stayed there for years and years longer, if I hadn't found it; perhaps stayed sunk underwater forever.

I've cleaned the tin up and I keep it on the mantelpiece at home with my coin-collection in it. I had to duck-dive later for another brick, and I got it all right, without being frightened at all; but it didn't seem to matter as much as coming up with the tin. I shall keep the tin as long as I live, and I might live to be a hundred.

ALFIE SANG

A TRUE STORY FROM LONDON

ALFIE was small, fat and four years old. Too small to go to school, too big to be kept safely in a pram. The flat Alfie lived in was small; on the 18th floor of a huge block of flats. He could only come down when his mother went shopping. And then there were only lift shafts, stone stairs, crowded streets, and if the lift was out of order there were 280 steps to climb.

Alfie liked noise – the shouting, stamping, banging kind. But the lady in the flat below did not like people stamping on her ceiling and the gentleman next door did not like shouting. Alfie liked sand and water. But sand scratched the floors and water made a mess. Sometimes Alfie cried.

One day Alfie's mother took him downstairs; not to go shopping, but to a hall near the flats. There were children everywhere. Sitting at tables, climbing up ladders, shouting, laughing, banging. There were swings and see-saws, blocks and tins, books and papers. Alfie did not know where to begin.

That afternoon, all the way back to the little flat on the 18th floor, Alfie sang. All his mother heard was a solemn, tuneless chant, but actually Alfie was singing of the glory of noise, of the stamping of feet, the banging of hammers, the shouting out loud. He sang of climbing and running and rolling; of the roughness of sand, the wetness of water and the rainbow beauty of paints, and of the pleasure of friends; and he sang because he knew he could go again the next day.

The place Alfie had found was one of the 80 city Playgroups organized by The Save the Children Fund in Great Britain, and there are 16 SCF Playgroups in the children's wards in United Kingdom hospitals. (You helped pay for them when you bought this book.)

BARBARA LEONIE PICARD

Tom Turnspit

THERE had been a state of simmering excitement in the castle kitchen ever since, in the late hours of the morning, one of the maidservants had run in, calling out that the players had come and were to perform in the great hall after supper. But when, later, my lord's steward had come to the kitchen to announce, in his usual self-important fashion, that my lord and lady had graciously given permission for all the castle servants to watch the play that evening, the excitement had risen to boiling within two minutes of his departure. After that, in the busy, bustling kitchen, the talk amongst the score of servants of every degree who worked there, had been of nothing but the players: for as a rule little entertainment ever came their way. First one of them and then another would be slipping out of the kitchen on some pretext or other, in the hope of catching a glimpse of the players, but with little success; though someone did claim to have seen two of them unloading from their cart one of the coffers which held whatever marvels it might be that players carried with them; while another swore to having seen their pony enjoying a well-earned rest and a feed in the castle stables.

It was so many years since a company of players had last visited the castle, that none of the younger servants had ever seen a play performed, and had little idea of what manner of folk players might be, or what form of entertainment they had to offer. Those of the older servants who claimed to have, at some time, seen players perform, and those others who professed to have more knowledge of the world found themselves being questioned avidly as to the ways and habits and appearance of players.

The most ignorant of all on the matter was undoubtedly the youngest and smallest of the scullions, Tom the found-ling, whose task it was to keep the spits turning with the dozens of fowl and the huge joints that were set to roast each day before the wide fireplaces. Even in winter, when warmth was welcome, it was no comfortable labour: in summer it was a torment. And when Tom was not turning the spits he was kept busy with all those other unpleasant tasks which every-one always left to him. Tom Turnspit, small and lean, his skin scorched brown as a wandering Egyptian's from long exposure to the flames, was the butt of the younger and live-lier servants and a scapegoat for all the rest.

The castle had been standing for about three hundred years, and the draughty great hall was on the first floor, above the huge kitchen. There was, of course, a comfortable modern wing, some fifty years old, with fine chambers for my lord and lady and their family, and a banqueting hall where, a good many years before Tom's unwanted birth, Queen Eliza-beth the First had been entertained for three whole days at an all but ruinous cost. But Tom had never set foot inside the new West Wing, and he could have counted on the fingers of two hands the times he had been in the great hall or any other upper room of the old building, and on the fingers of one hand the times that he had gone beyond the castle walls, to the nearby village with its church, its alehouse, and its watermill. For Tom's own world was bounded by the kitchen walls; within them he worked all day, and in a draughty corner, on a heap of straw and rags, he slept at night.

On this fine early autumn day he became aware of the players' arrival and saw the stir it caused, and he wondered at it, for he had never heard of folk called players and had no idea what they could be. He knew, though, that it would be useless for him to ask, for no one would bother to tell him; and it was more than likely that he would have his ears boxed for asking questions about matters which were not his concern. But he listened to what was being said all around him, and in this way he learnt several conflicting facts: that players were like mummers; that they were not, for they were different and far better than mummers; that they sang songs and begged for pence; that they did not sing, but told stories about kings and queens, and pretended to be those kings and queens while they were telling the stories; that they danced, wearing strange clothing, upon stilts and swords; that they did not dance but juggled instead with knives and balls and platters. Tom also overheard Simon, who was usually respected by all for being able to read and write, declare several times, forcibly and heatedly, to different people, that players were rogues and vagabonds who should be whipped from any place where they dared to show their brazen faces; but Tom decided that this might perhaps be discounted, since everyone else jeered at Simon for a scurvy, spoilsport puritan, who was talking nonsense.

It was all very bewildering to Tom, but also very marvel-

lous; and when, along with the others, he heard from the lips
of the steward himself that all the servants might see the
players, he could hardly believe his luck. And, hardly believ-
ing it, he thought he would do best to make sure of it. Timidly
he approached the head cook, who, fortunately, had seemed
in a good mood all that morning, and asked if he, too, might
see the players in the great hall. He was immediately afraid
that he had been mistaken about the cook's mood, when he
heard him bellow in reply, 'What's that I hear? You, you
idle brat, you want to see the players? Most certainly you
shall not.'

Though terrified, Tom's longing to see the players was such
that he dared a second appeal. 'But, please, sir, Master Bolton
said my lord had told him all the servants might see the
players. All of them, sir.'

Tom had, in fact, not been mistaken. The cook was in a
very good mood that morning. After glaring at Tom in silence
for a full half-minute, so that Tom began to tremble, he burst
into a loud guffaw. 'So that's what my lord said, is it? "All
the servants and make sure that Tom Turnspit is not forgotten." Lackwit, do you think my lord even knows there's
an ugly brat named Tom in his kitchen? To be sure he does
not! And if he has never heard of you, he cannot mean you
to go to the great hall and see the players, can he?'

Poor Tom had no idea of how to answer this. Miserably he
watched the cook begin to laugh again, heard others join in
his mirth, and believed that all was lost. But when the cook
had laughed his fill, he said, 'Very well, Master Thomas
Turnspit, valued servant of my lord, you shall see the players
this evening – but only if you work hard and I can find no
fault with you all day. Now be off with you and back to your
tasks.' He hurried Tom on his way with a clout, and Tom,
incredulous and overjoyed, fled back to the spits.

Never one who dared to shirk, Tom surpassed even himself

that day, working every second, and working enough for three; the whole time in spirits which at one moment reached the heights of joyful anticipation, and at the next fell to despairing depths at the thought that he might in some way be found to have trespassed, and so lose the promised reward. But all went well, and at last the time came when the servants, in chattering groups, friend by cheerful friend, began to make their way to the great hall. Tom's heart was hammering with excitement, his eyes were bright with eagerness, and his whole being was alive with an unfamiliar emotion to which, had he been asked, he could not have given a name, since he had never before experienced happiness. He was making to follow three of the other lads from the kitchen – he would never have dared to join them and walk beside them, nor, indeed, would they have permitted it; and he was beneath the arch of the doorway when the head cook's voice roared out at him, 'Tom, you good for nothing, where do you think you're going? Come here at once.'

The cook's good mood had not lasted quite long enough. Not fifteen minutes before, he had fallen out with the cellarer and had had the worst of their argument; now he was looking for a victim on whom he might avenge his discomfiture. Upon Tom's stammered 'You said I might see the players if you found no fault with me today, sir. You have not –' the cook broke in furiously, 'And now I have changed my mind. The great hall is no place for a misbegotten beggar's brat. You shall stay here where you belong.' He struck out at Tom and, his rancour somewhat appeased, strode away up to the great hall.

Tom hardly felt the blow which sent him sprawling, and he was unaware of the bruising flagstones on which he fell; all he knew, and all he could feel or think of, was that he would not see the players.

*

In the great hall of the castle, where at one end a stage had been improvised for the players, the play had begun. To Martin, in his role of the Good Angel, had been allotted the lines – Prologue, linking narratory passages and Epilogue – intended to be spoken by Chorus. At first, as he had stepped forward from behind the screens which had been set up to mask the players' entrances and conceal the archway to the back-stairs up which they had to come, he had been a little nervous: not afraid of failure – he was too certain of his skill for that – but cautious and ready to adapt his perform-ance to the mood of the spectators, as was wise when facing an audience whose tastes and temper were unknown. Yet there had been no sign of tenseness as his first words had rung out confidently, and the sweet sound of his clear, high voice had filled the hall.

> Not marching in the fields of Thrasimene,
> Where Mars did mate the warlike Carthagens . . .

He did not fear the responsibility of being the one to speak the opening lines and set the play upon its course, for he en-joyed the challenge offered by his rivals for the spectators' attention: ale-mug or wine-cup, flirtatious wench or lovely lady, ribald jesting or scholarly discussion; and when he handed on an eager and receptive audience to the player who was the next to speak, he rejoiced in the pride he could always feel in something well achieved.

By the time his tenth line had been spoken, he knew that he had all their eyes and ears: the spectators' attention was his to keep safely until the closing lines of the Prologue, ready to be handed over to Master Banbury.

> Nothing so sweet as magic is to him,
> Which he prefers before his chiefest bliss:
> And this the man that in his study sits.

As the beautiful tones fell silent there was noisy and appreciative applause. Martin bowed deeply and, before it ceased and the spectators could begin to comment amongst each other on his appearance and performance, and thus leave the player who followed him to win their attention all over again, he slipped behind the screens to where Master Banbury, leader of the company of players, was waiting, garbed as a scholar, an open book in his hands. He nodded approvingly to Martin, whispered, 'Well done, lad,' then paced gravely from behind the screens, reading in his book as he walked, and sat down upon the bench which had been placed ready for him, a pile of three or four more books set to one end of it, to represent a study. After reading a moment or two further, he looked up and started on his long first speech:

> Settle thy studies, Faustus, and begin
> To sound the depth of that thou wilt profess ...

The Tragical History of the Life and Death of Dr Faustus, by Christopher Marlowe, was away to a promising start.

A small chamber near the foot of the secondary stairway which twisted down from the end of the great hall had been allotted to the players as a tiring-room. In the confusion of costumes, properties and bodies half-clad or strangely bedizened, Martin, helped by Robin, the younger and smaller of the two other boys in the company, now attired as a devil, removed his angel's wig and halo, wings and white robe. Underneath he already had on the patched trunk-hose of Wagner, the poor scholar who was servant to Dr Faustus. In spite of extensive cuts to the text and the omission of a number of characters, everyone in the company except Master Banbury as Faustus and young Master Kenton – who was Martin's own especial friend among them all and was playing Mephistopheles – was obliged to take several parts. Martin himself, beside his combination of the roles of the Good

Angel and Chorus, was playing Wagner, Helen of Troy and one of the Seven Deadly Sins. The playwright's not having made provision for quite such stringent economy in the presentation of his work, had brought about two extremely quick changes for Martin. To see him safely through these, Master Kenton, who had a turn for words, had augmented Marlowe's verse by the addition of some score or so, and a dozen, lines respectively – something which he was not infrequently called upon to do on behalf of one playwright or another.

While Martin was hurriedly putting on Wagner's threadbare scholar's coat he was also trying to answer everyone's questions as to how the Prologue had been received, and what opinion he had formed of the spectators, and a handful of other matters. His change completed, he told Robin to come with him up to the hall, bringing the Good Angel's costume, because the first of his two quickest changes was due to be made after his first short scene as Wagner, and there would be no time for climbing down the break-neck, twisting stairway to the tiring-room and up again. 'I'll carry the wings, and you can bring the rest. And for heaven's sake take care you do not tangle the wig or set the halo awry while going up the stairs, you imp of Satan,' he warned, his familiar appellation for Robin sounding, for once, appropriate. Robin grimaced horribly and put out his tongue, then skipped away neatly as Martin aimed a good-natured cuff at him. Picking up the Good Angel's wings of canvas-covered framework sewn with hundreds of dyed or gilded hens' feathers, Martin noticed a loose feather hanging by a single thread: there was no time to deal with it now; it would have to be stitched when the costumes were repacked. In the doorway he turned back and called to Master Kenton, 'Those stairs, Will, they are dark enough already. This piece goes on for ever : it will be as black as the pit on the stairway long before we're done. We'll need torches if we are not to break our necks hurrying on them.'

Master Kenton, knotting a cord around the Greyfriar's habit which was Mephistopheles' disguise, grinned and waved a hand at him. 'I'll see to it. Now, for the love of heaven, make haste, or you'll miss your cue. Good luck !'

Martin did not miss his cue; moreover, aided by Robin, he managed his change back to the Good Angel in a remarkably short time, all things considered.

The play progressed, well received by the spectators at every point, and neared its closing scenes. Torches were lit and set around the now darkening hall. During another rapid change behind the screens Martin donned a farthingale and a very handsome – even if a trifle worn – gown of crimson brocade over Wagner's hose. Around his neck was a starched ruffle, on his head a gilt crown atop a wig of the popular saffron shade; while from his shoulders hung the silver-embroidered velvet cloak which was always worn by royalty in every play that boasted regal characters. Then, as Helen of Troy, Martin was led ceremoniously on stage by Mephistopheles. With the eye which was turned from the spectators, Master Kenton winked at him, murmuring out of that corner of his mouth which they could not see, 'That should please them ! I'll wager not Helen herself looked lovelier !'

Slowly, with grace and regal dignity – for, though flighty, Helen had been a great queen, he reminded himself – Martin walked across the stage and was conscious of the buzz of admiration that stirred the spectators. No hard-won triumph, this one, he was thinking. Helen was the easiest of characters to play if one had the looks: Marlowe had written no speeches for her. He disappeared again behind the screens to await Helen's second entrance. He did not have to listen for a cue, because Mephistopheles would fetch him once again, so he was free to relax and enjoy a brief rest.

The play was going well, he thought, pleased. And he himself was doing none too ill, with his several parts and the costume changes they involved; not ill at all, considering it was a play with only two short speaking parts for women – neither of which he was playing – and was, therefore, a far from satisfactory play, regarded from his point of view. Though it did offer some good practice for the future, he reflected, since there would be not much longer before his voice broke and he could play no more woman's parts. Well, he had no fear of being unwanted in the company. Unlike some boy players he did not owe his success merely to looks and voice alone. He would, he knew, when the day came, play the hero with as much skill and success and satisfaction as he had played the heroine. Will Kenton – the best player in the company; better even than old Master Banbury – had been training him for two years now against that day. And while he stepped straight from playing women to playing gay young lovers and the like, Crispin and little Robin would be doing their best with the rôles which he would have bequeathed them – and failing to achieve a tithe of his success. It was no easy life, there was much hard work, he admitted that. But it was a good life and he would not change it for any other in the world; yet it had been mere chance that had brought him to it. Deliberately Martin turned his mind back to the present. He always preferred not to remember those first seven lonely years which had ended for him on that thrice blessed day when the players had come by, and, struck by the beauty of the unloved orphan, had relieved his harsh foster parents of a burden they had rejoiced to lose.

The grey Franciscan figure appeared beside him to rouse him from his day dreams. From beneath the cowl Will's face grinned at him. 'Come, it's time for their second chance to gape at you. I trust they know how privileged they are !'

They took hands, and with fiendish triumph in this latest

step in the downfall of the unfortunate Faustus, Mephistopheles led Helen of Troy from behind the screens; bowing
over her hand, as he released it, in a manner more suited to
a courtier than an apparent friar.

> Was this the face that launched a thousand ships,
> And burnt the topless towers of Ilium? ...

queried Dr Faustus, in Master Banbury's most ringing tones;
and, every inch a queen of ancient days, Helen walked slowly
towards him, the first faint traces of a beguiling smile beginning to curve her lips.

And so the play moved on to its grim ending. Abandoned
by the Good Angel, to an accompaniment of thunder – cym-
bals crashed noisily behind the screens – a vainly pleading
Faustus was dragged off to hell by two devils – one of them
rather small and shrill – whose bloodcurdling howls and
fiendish laughter amply compensated for their lack of num-
bers. Then Chorus, still in the person of the Good Angel,
gravely pronounced his final moralizing words: the play was
over and, from the applause, an undeniable success.

*

Of the four who had remained in the castle kitchen only old
Samuel had a mind at peace, nodding and snoring on a stool
so close beside the fire that it seemed as though he were seeking, on this mild autumn evening, to store up in his twisted,
aching old body as much warmth as he might against the icy
winter days that lay ahead.

Tom squatted on the straw, thin arms about thin knees,
staring at the floor and hearing Simon the puritan, who sat
at a table, his greasy, well-thumbed Bible open before him,
half reading and half declaiming in his grating voice passages
which seemed to him appropriate to the sin of play-acting
and the fate of those who concerned themselves with it. Tom

felt as though every word were being directed at him, and him alone, because he had wanted so much to see the players.

Her feet shuffling on the flagstones, Mad Meg went up and down the length of the kitchen, singing a plaintive lullaby to her cradled, empty arms. Twelve years before, so Tom had heard the tale told, Meg had been a fair young widow with a son. One day the child had wandered off alone and fallen into the deep millpool and there been drowned; and from grief Meg had gone out of her mind. She was a good dairymaid, and hardworking, and she harmed no one; but all the while she worked, and whenever her work was done, she would talk or sing quietly to herself without pause – only it was not to herself that she spoke and crooned, but to her child. Sometimes, but rarely, she would remember that the boy was dead, and cry out against the cruel waters of the millpool.

She was the only person Tom could have named, who had never, by word or deed, caused him hurt. Living in a withdrawn world of her own, she was usually unaware of him and never spoke to him save on those infrequent occasions when the tangible world outside her became, for a little while, as real to her as that other world in her own mind; then she would seek him out as being the youngest of the scullions and warn him with terrifyingly convincing earnestness never to go near the millpool, lest he should fall in and be drowned.

Hearing her now, he thought – as he had thought before, and more than once – how strange it was that God, Who was said to be good and just, should have permitted a beloved only child to drown, bringing his mother a sorrow that stole her wits away; while he, Tom, whom no one wanted, lived and flourished to be despised and beaten. Meg's tender lullaby, no less than her sorrow, seemed to Tom to reproach him for living and breathing when her own child was dead and gone. Good Mistress Meg, he implored her in his heart, do not blame me, for today I would so willingly change places with your son.

It is curious how, day in and day out, for year after year, one can accept misery, and endure, and exist without hope; and never think to seek a means of escape from one's wretched condition. And then one day there will come but a single instance of a new affliction – perhaps small enough in itself in comparison with its precursors – that can, in a moment, break one, as not all the accumulated and accustomed trials had been able to do. Such an affliction had that day fallen upon Tom; and where before he had, like an animal, accepted tribulation blindly, and endured, he now saw the full extent of the hopelessness of his existence and believed he could endure no longer.

Yet would he find the courage he needed, he wondered, picturing himself stealing from the castle and running, running down the track to the village, and so to the watermill. In imagination he stood on the brink of the pool above the dark water and felt it call to him.

Tomorrow, he promised himself, tomorrow I shall have the courage, and tomorrow I shall be free.

The play being over, the servants began to return to the kitchen, most of them excitedly talking over the evening's entertainment. Tom could not bear to know what those marvels were, which he had missed. Afraid of overhearing of some delight which had been denied to him, he stole away, out of the kitchen and along a poorly lighted passage, caring not where he went so long as he was beyond the reach of the cheerful chattering. His steps soon dragged to a standstill. By this time tomorrow, he thought, the waters of the mill-pool would have swallowed him – but he would have not even a Mad Meg to mourn for him. Of a sudden overwhelmingly desolate, he dropped to his knees, covered his face with his hands and burst into tears. Crouched forward he wept brokenheartedly. After some moments, above the sound of his own sobs, he caught the sound of voices. Always wary and over-expectant of blame or punishment, he looked up quickly. Coming towards him along the passage was a small, dark figure, carrying a lighted torch. He heard it speak shrilly and clearly – too clearly for him to have misheard the words which shocked him with swift terror.

'I hope they've thought to give us all a large tankard of ale apiece. Dragging sinners off to hell is thirsty work.'

Transfixed with fear, Tom watched the dark figure approach. Too afraid to attempt to fly from it, he crouched against the foot of the wall in the shadows. Suddenly the figure began to skip up and down, flourishing the flaring torch and chanting in bloodcurdling accents, 'Dragging sinners off to hell, off to hell, off to hell, dragging sinners off to hell is thirsty work.'

The dark figure was perhaps no taller than Tom would have been, had he been standing and not cowering in its path. As it came even nearer, Tom saw by the torchlight that it was pitch black from top to toe; and that upon its head – he was able to see quite plainly now, shock having dammed the flow of his tears – upon its head, dear God protect us, were two horns. Flourishing the torch and still chanting its ghastly song, the creature spun neatly round on its heels three times, setting its own and other shadows to a horrid dancing on the walls; and, as it turned – oh, worse and worse ! – Tom could see it had a tail.

At that moment Tom became aware that behind it was a taller, paler figure, which now spoke for the first time. 'You imp of Satan, stop jigging about and making such a din, or it's you who'll be picked up and tossed back into hell, where you belong.'

The little black devil – for poor Tom had now no doubts as to what the creature was – gave a wail of extreme anguish

and cried out, in the most supplicating tones, 'Your pardon, your pardon, I beseech you, great master! Look not so fierce on me! Oh, spare me! Ugly hell gape not! I will be good and quiet, I swear I will. See how quiet I am!' Holding the torch high, the devil advanced on tiptoe, with long silent strides, and it was almost upon the terrified Tom before it noticed him in the shadows. With a startled squeal, it retreated. 'Oh! There's someone there, on the floor. Look!'

The taller figure came forward. 'Bring the torch! Why, it's only a boy, no bigger than you. That's nothing to be scared of.'

The torch, held out by the devil, showed Tom's tear-stained face and reddened eyes. 'What's wrong? Why do you weep?'

The clear, high voice was like no other that Tom had ever heard. He stared up at the tall being which seemed to tower above him. Slim and straight, all dazzling gold and white in the torchlight: spotless white robe, golden hair encircled by a ring of fire above a serene and lovely face, and, just glimpsed over its shoulders, glowing with gold and rainbow colours – yes, surely those were wings? 'You . . . you must be an angel,' faltered Tom.

'To be sure I am an angel: and a good angel at that!' The angel smiled at him, and Tom had never dreamt that any face could be so beautiful. Without taking his eyes from the countenance which so graciously looked down on him, he gestured with his hand and asked fearfully, 'And that other: what is he?'

The angel's smile deepened and he gave a little, melodious laugh – just such a laugh as one might have expected from an angel, had one ever presumed to imagine an angel laughing – and said, 'Oh, he! He is the blackest and wickedest of all the smaller devils sent to plague mankind. But you have no cause to fear his mischief, for I have overcome him and he is now my slave.'

The blackest and wickedest of all the smaller devils made a sound which, in a human being, would have been an exclamation of indignant protest; but which, Tom supposed, must be a devil's way of expressing sorrow for his fate.

The angel spared no glance for the defeated devil, but continued to smile down at Tom. 'Did you not see the play, then?' he asked.

Tom shook his head. 'No. In the end he would not let me, though he had said I might.'

'Who would not let you?'

'Master Walters, my lord's head cook. He's so often cruel and unfair to me. So, too, are many of the others.' In a more matter of fact voice, Tom added in explanation, 'You see, I'm only Tom Turnspit of the kitchen, so no one's ever kind to me.'

'But what of your father and mother, Tom? Are they, also, servants here? And are they not kind?'

'I never had a mother or a father. I'm a foundling.'

The angel was silent for a few moments before replying; then he said, 'I am sorry. It's a bad thing to be an orphan. I know: for I, too, had no father or mother.'

Tom, who had begun to feel reassured by the angel's apparent benevolence, now forgot even more of his fear in surprise at the angel's words. At first he could only stare up in wonder; and then he understood. Of course, how should an angel, begotten in heaven of flame and light and glory, have parents like mortal men? Yet how strange it was that an angel should, like a poor scullion, regret having no parents. But even while he puzzled over this, it came to him that a deficiency which he shared with one of God's glorious angels could be no shame at all. To be in a like condition to an immortal angel, even if only in this one respect, was cause for pride, not shame.

'How old are you?' he heard the angel ask.

'I do not know. No one has ever told me.'

'Stand up then, so I may see you.' The angel held out a hand to him and Tom wondered whether he dared touch the hand, to kiss it. Timidly he raised his own hand a little way towards the angel's; then, too awed to complete his gesture, was about to draw his hand back when he found it in the angel's grasp and himself being raised to his feet. The angel looked him up and down thoughtfully, then pronounced, 'About ten years old, I'd guess.' He went on, encouragingly, 'That is ten bad years behind you already. You're well past half-way to better days: not many of the bad years remain for you. You'll not be hectored and tormented for ever, you know – though now it may seem so. You'll grow older, and quickly, too: from hour to hour we ripe and ripe. One day you'll find yourself as tall and strong as anyone, with a fine big beard to bristle at them, and a fine deep voice for growling at them. And when that day comes they'll not dare to cross you or to. . . . Or to pluck off your beard or call you villain or break your pate across ! Indeed, the shoe may well be on the other foot, and it be you who'll be hectoring and tormenting them. Try to remember that, whenever things go ill for you: you'll find it helps, I promise you. And one thing more, and by no means the least: show yourself a little respect and admiration. For the more highly you rate yourself, the more highly others will rate you. Do you think you'll be able to remember so many things without me to prompt you?'

Tom, still awed, but at the same time exhilarated, nodded. 'I'll try to remember – always,' he whispered.

The angel turned his head to glance over his shoulder. He raised a hand to his left wing and brought it away holding something which he offered to Tom with a friendly, and almost human, chuckle. 'A keepsake to aid your memory. Lay it safely by and look at it whenever you need to remind yourself of the good angelic counsel you've been given today.'

Reverently Tom took from the angel's outstretched hand a single golden feather, stiff and glittering. Wonderingly he gazed at it.

'Now it must be good night, Thomas Turnspit. Farewell, and good luck to you.' The angel snapped his fingers to call the little black devil who was stifling a wide yawn with the hand that was not holding the torch.

While Tom was yet staring at the golden feather, the angel and the little devil had turned a corner; by the time Tom looked up, not even the light of their torch could be seen. Had it not been for the golden feather he held, they might never have been there, or he might have believed it a dream – or rather, he might, had it not been for both the golden feather and the angel's counsel, which he was never, never going to forget. And it was true: they had been there. A fierce joy suddenly rose in him. God was, after all, good and just, and He had not forgotten him. He had sent him an angel with a message of hope. For poor, slighted Tom Turnspit had he done this. Not to my lord, not to my lady, not to any of their sons or daughters, not to Bible-reading Simon who talked so much of Him, not to Master Bolton nor to Master Walters, and not even to poor, suffering Mad Meg – but to Tom Turnspit had He sent His angel.

Standing there with the feather in his hand, and hope taking root, to grow and blossom, in his heart, Tom promised himself that no one else should ever learn of the favour which had been granted to him alone. It was his own great secret; and so long as it remained inviolate and his alone, so long would he be as strong as – and stronger than – all others who did not share his knowledge and had not been granted a like experience. As for the feather, no eyes but his should ever share the sight of it. He would find a scrap of cloth to wrap about it, he decided, and a length of thread to knot it fast, and he would hang it safely about his neck, an amulet for his protection, and never leave it off.

In a little while he started back for the kitchen, carefully carrying his treasure. His step was firm now and confident, and he walked hopefully towards the future; for, no matter what others might do or say to him now, with his great secret knowledge he, poor Tom Turnspit – no, not poor Tom Turnspit, but God's own chosen Thomas – God's own chosen Thomas was, by His grace, the equal, and more than the equal, of any man alive.

BOY WITH A KITE

A TRUE STORY FROM HONG KONG

CHAN YIN had a secret. Twice it had been discovered, once by an older boy and once by his mother. Each time it was destroyed and he had to start all over again. Now it was safely hidden under a pile of rubbish in a corner of the shack of tin and sacking that was his home.

It was a kite, made from bits and pieces carefully salvaged from the city's gutters and garbage tins. It had taken him months to make and the day it was finished he played truant from school and spent a blissful afternoon flying it in a field outside the city. When at last he was tired it was too dark for him to find his way home, so he slept in a doorway.

Next morning he went home to discover that the entire row of shacks where he lived had disappeared. In those twenty-four hours the buildings had been demolished and there was no one left to tell him where his family had gone.

Poor little Chan Yin wandered the streets of the city all day looking for a familiar face. And that night, still clutching his kite, he cried himself to sleep under a bridge.

Next morning he was still wandering the streets, dreadfully hungry. Then he came to a playground. Inside crowds of cheerful children ran and climbed and shouted. He talked to them through the palings and they told him that they came here every day, and that, not only did they play, but they had a meal before they went home.

A bell rang and they lined up to go inside. Chan could smell the food and felt weak. He slipped through the gate, joined the line, and took a seat. Then one of the boys spotted him. What was he doing there? He didn't belong to the playground. A large bowl, steaming and fragrant, was placed before the boy at his side. 'You can have my kite,' he whispered to the big boy, 'But don't say anything.' And before he could change his mind a bowl was placed in front of him and blissfully he buried his small nose in the fragrance. Quickly, silently he ate. All too soon the bowl was empty but he was still hungry. He looked around. There was still a queue of boys waiting to sit down. A queue that went right outside the door. Chan slipped out the door, around the side of the building, and attached himself to the end of the queue.

Once again he was sitting at the table; once again he was burying his nose in a fragrant bowl. But before he could lift his chopsticks to his lips he was discovered. He was betrayed. By the big boy who had his kite. 'He was here before; he doesn't belong here; he is an impostor.'

But Chan Yin's story had a happy ending. The Save the Children Fund found his parents and made a place for him in a hostel for boys where he can go to school and play safely.

And what was the first thing Chan did when he had settled in? There he was, poking around in the dustbins and in odd corners for scraps and bits to make a new kite.

You helped to pay for Chan's soup when you bought this book.

BARBARA SOFTLY

Master Ghost and I

'FIVE years is a long time,' said Nathaniel Dodds, my
father's steward, his eyes sweeping contemptuously over my
travel-stained clothing, the jack-boots and buff coat of a
Parliamentary officer in the New Model Army.

'You ran away from home when you were thirteen rather
than study to enter the Church and so serve King Charles,'
he added unnecessarily, for he was only too familiar with the
circumstances which had made my family disown me.

'I would have fought for the King had I been allowed,' I
replied. 'My brothers did so – I had no choice, only that of
entering the Church, and I did what any boy of spirit would
have done, ran away and made myself safe from pursuit by
joining the rebels.'

Five years earlier it would have been a hot-tempered answer; but five years is a long time and I had learnt much

77

rising from a fanatical schoolboy to a captain in charge of men older than myself.

'You caused your parents much distress,' snapped Dodds.

'And what of my distress?' I asked. 'Why should a boy's life be moulded to suit his parents' whim? The Church was not for me. If by exiling me and making me homeless they have been unhappy, they are to blame for it, not I.'

They were hard words which came from a heart steeled to live without home or kindred in the face of the destruction of bitter Civil War.

Dropping my hat and gloves on the floor, I sat down uninvited in the chair opposite the steward's desk.

'I came as soon as I received your message,' I went on. 'Your reason for giving me two days' hard riding was not, I believe, to speak of my parents –'

'No. As far as your parents are concerned, you no longer exist.'

So much for any hope of reconciliation. Dodds turned to his table on which was a roll of parchment held flat by a weight.

'Your father had one brother, Edward Knapton,' he began abruptly. 'A man known for his wealth and loyalty to the King – he fought with him in his campaign in the West Country. Like many other soldiers, when he went to war he made a will in which he left his considerable fortune to your father, your brothers – and to you,' he added darkly. 'Naturally your name was removed five years ago.'

'Naturally,' I nodded.

Suddenly the weight was flung aside, the parchment seized and Dodds' voice rang out in anger.

'A short while ago Edward Knapton destroyed that first will, and made this – this travesty of a document,' the parchment shook, 'and left his entire fortune to you, you alone.'

He flung the document back on the desk and faced me wrathfully. 'Why? Why?'

Years of training kept my indifferent mask.

'No doubt he knew the others were rich enough,' I replied. 'After all, I have only my captain's pay.'

'Pah! He hated Cromwell and his Roundheads, and you for serving them. No, he was mad, mad when he made this; mad, sick or frightened – and if I had not known for a fact that you were two hundred miles away at the time, I should have blamed you for it.'

He turned to a small chest and drew out a bag of coins.

'What's done is done and there's no more to be said. Take this now, you know where to find me when you want more and after the house is sold –'

'What house?' I asked.

'His house – a new house,' he barked, naming a part of the West Country which had suffered badly from the plunderings of both sides during the wars. 'It was finished this spring. He planned to live in it at once but – you'll not be needing it, always on the move. You left one Royalist home and this will only be another.'

The taunt stung; and the ready assumption that I neither wanted nor needed the house roused my obstinate nature, though I was little inclined to be saddled with the property.

'I may not wish to sell it,' I replied. 'I'll see it first. In any case the servants may not wish to serve a rebel master after a Royalist one.'

'There are no servants!' he whispered, a look of fear coming into his eyes. 'No one will stay there – the place is haunted. Even your uncle was driven by its evil –'

'Haunted!' I laughed. 'A house not a year old with a ghost! Is it Master Bricklayer fallen from the scaffolding who tumbles his bricks down the chimneys every windy night, or Master Ghost the –'

'Fool! Conceited, young fool!' Master Dodds swung on me a white passionate face. 'Heaven be praised you never entered the Church after all – the supernatural is to be feared not mocked.'

Hurriedly he gave me a bunch of keys from the small coffer.

'Return them when you have changed your mind.'

'Maybe I'll not change my mind,' I smiled. 'For perhaps Master Ghost and I will become well acquainted.'

Forty-eight hours later, on a dull summer evening of steady wind and cloud, I stood surveying my inheritance, or what could be seen of its chimneys above high, uncut hawthorn hedges and a massive gateway.

Behind, lay the overgrown track which had led from the road; to the left, smoke from a tree-lined hollow betrayed hidden cottages, and to the right fold upon fold of wooded hillsides. If it had not been for that smoke I should have thought the whole countryside deserted, for not one villager had I met in the last three miles of my journey. Everything was unnaturally quiet, only the wind in the hedge and the chink of the bridle – I felt I was being watched.

Having tethered my animal, I thrust one of Dodds' keys into the new lock and although it turned easily, it needed the weight of my shoulder to force the gate backwards far enough to allow me to squeeze into my own estate. There I remained, stupidly bewildered and gaping. There was no smooth drive – nothing but waist-high grass bending to the everlasting wind; the house, stables, mature lime trees seemed to have dropped from the skies into a vast hayfield. Blank windows gaped back and little wisps of straw pattered along the newly laid terrace beneath them.

There is untold desolation about an empty house, desolation and stillness. Yet here there was no stillness and the desolation was crying aloud with the wind that brushed the lime branches to the ground and swept the dried blossom in never-ending motion; a wind of lost crying voices – truly a wind of ghosts.

Slowly I waded through the grasses to the edge of the terrace, my hand on my sword.

'Will you be wanting anything, sir?'

I spun round, but it was no ghost that pushed itself through the bushes at the side of the house. It was a man whose eyes filled with hatred at the nearness of my Parliamentary buff coat. He carried a scythe, swung aloft like an ancient battle-axe.

'I'm Mallett,' he began. 'Ned Mallett, and I be here to cut the grass. Master only wanted it cut once a year.' His eyes raked my uniform again. 'You're a soldier – and as we don't hold with soldiers in these parts, you'd best be off before we make you. And take your men off, too.'

'I am alone,' I snapped, annoyed at my former fear. 'This property is now mine. Your master was my uncle.'

'That's as maybe,' he growled. 'You're a soldier and we've had enough of soldiery whether they be King's men or Parliament's. We don't want no more of your trampling our crops, burning, frightening our womenfolk, taking all and paying nothing. We fought you once with pitchforks and clubs and we'll fight you again.'

He was right. Villagers in that area had been called the Clubmen because, sickened by the plunder of war from both Royalist and Roundhead, they had banded together to fight a common enemy and no bribes from either side had ever won them over.

'You be off,' he muttered. 'Maybe Master Knapton were a soldier, but he wouldn't stay here neither. Worried out of his wits, he was, though it weren't us what scared him. Might have been though, if the devil hadn't done it for us. "Ned Mallett" he said to me –'

'Never you mind what he said to you,' I interrupted, my temper rising. 'Whoever stabled his horses and cooked his food can do it for me now. I intend to stay the night, so be off down to the village and find someone to light the fires and air the linen.'

Mallett's eyes wavered from mine, shifting to something over my left shoulder.

'My Missus'll do it,' he said, suddenly amenable. He jerked the scythe to the ground and strode off towards the cottages in the hollow.

I turned quickly and with an exclamation of annoyance saw another prying villager standing watching behind me. Although it was only a boy of about thirteen I was beginning to think I should sleep sounder with my hostile neighbours on the other side of a locked door.

'Who are you?' I barked.

'R-Roger,' he stammered.

'And you live here, too, I suppose?'

'S-sort of.'

We looked each other up and down.

'You're a soldier,' he said.

'A captain of a troop of horse. Before that I served under Waller in most of his campaigns; and I have been a soldier for the past five years.'

I rolled out the words waiting for the inevitable disapproval. It did not come. The boy was staring at me with an odd mixture of incredulity and admiration.

His hair was cropped shorter than mine had ever been; he was wearing a shabby doublet and breeches of a faded blue-grey. But none of his clothes seemed shabby with the wear of work, rather, they were faded with disuse, the lace of his shirt yellowed, dust lines in the creases – and it seemed probable that he was dressed in a discarded suit of my uncle.

'You knew Master Edward Knapton who lived here?' I asked.

'He came a short while ago. I met him then,' was the quick reply.

'And he gave you those clothes?'

A glimmer of astonishment showed on the boy's face as he glanced at his doublet.

'They – came from the chest at the foot of his bed,' he explained. Then eagerly, 'Why are you here? You're a soldier and there's no fighting now.'

'Because the house is mine.' They will soon understand that, I thought. 'I am Edward Knapton's nephew, John Knapton, who –'

'John Knapton!' He broke in excitedly. 'You are John Knapton? But – but you're a soldier, a captain – no one would ever have dreamed you were a Roundhead soldier as well –'

'As well as what?' I asked.

He flushed, shrugging his shoulders.

'As well as being – being –'

'As well as being the nephew of a loyal subject of the King,' I finished for him.

'That's as good a reason as any,' he laughed, seemingly relieved.

His laughter was cheering after Mallett's welcome. I liked the boy with his disarming friendliness and quaint clipped way of speaking, different from Mallett's broad vowels or my slight country drawl. Turning away, I crossed the terrace to open the door at the front of the house, and boy Roger padded after me. As the lock clicked and the door swung inwards, he wriggled under my arm to stand staring in awe at the dark, musty hall.

'Look,' he whispered, his voice quivering with the excitement of a great discovery. 'It's new, so new! The panelling, the floor, the banisters.' And he darted away to smooth his hands over the freshly carved woodwork.

'Of course it's new,' I said. 'It was only finished recently. Surely you saw it when Master Knapton was here?'

'I – I didn't come in,' he murmured with an effort, seeming to check his eagerness.

From then on, wherever I went, Roger followed in silence through the living-room, kitchens and up the stairs, his eyes burning with curiosity, his fingers caressing objects with an almost loving familiarity, until I paused to open one of the windows in what I guessed was my uncle's bedroom.

With a soft exclamation, Roger slipped to his knees to gaze at the linen chest at the foot of the bed.

'It's unbelievable – but it's the same,' he whispered.

'If it's the one from which Master Knapton took your suit I'm not surprised it's the same,' I said. 'But as you did not come indoors when he was here, I don't see how you can recognize it.'

His eyes dropped guiltily from mine.

'The date is carved on the lid, I expect,' I pointed. 'Yes, 1600. No doubt he had it as a young man. It's old now, nearly fifty years.'

'Fifty years – that's not old!' Roger protested. 'It won't look like that in three hundred years, that I know.'

'Neither will you,' I retorted.

This time his eyes met mine fearlessly, and through the open window I was conscious of the wind tap-tapping the lime branches on the terrace below.

' "*Tempus edax rerum*",' I quoted abruptly.

'Eh?' he started. 'That's Latin, isn't it? I don't know any. I don't take Latin at my school.'

'Latin, boy, of course it's Latin!' I exclaimed, but held back further comment. For all I knew he might be some local lad my uncle had befriended who was trying to hide his ignorance by blaming his schoolmaster.

'Time, the devourer of all things, is a fair translation,' I explained; and the little lost ghost voices of the wind came crying into my uncle's room.

I turned quickly from the strange look on the face of the boy at my feet, heard the clatter on the flags as Mallett led my horse to the stables, and strode to the head of the stairs. Uneasy, impatient, I hardly knew, only that the atmosphere of the house and the people I had met oppressed me.

Who was Roger? A spy sent by the Clubmen to gain my confidence and then at a given signal help to rid them of the unwanted soldier owner of the property? I had been a fool to admit I was alone, a fool to leave my pistols on my saddle, now in Mallett's hands – and a fool to come. No doubt Dodds was right. The house was haunted by pitchforks and ill-will.

One backward glance at Roger showed me that disturbing smile. I hastened down the stairs, past the kitchens where Mallett's wife called – 'There's bread and cheese and ale for your supper. I'll make up the beds and then you must shift for yourself. I'll not stay after dark in this God forsaken place.'

God forsaken place – yes. I flung my hat and gloves on the settle in the living-room and sat at the table in the window, staring over the unending grass in the swiftly falling darkness. No doubt by morning, if I still lived, I should be ready to return the keys.

And apparently Roger was to remain the night with me. Without turning my head I was able to watch him where he sprawled on the settle engrossed in examining the stitching on my gloves – future spoil from a dead man, I thought.

'It's dark in here,' I snapped.

'Dark?' he started in alarm. 'I'll switch the light on.'

He sprang to the door, his fingers pressing the wall. Then he paused, his hand slipping awkwardly to his side.

'What is it?' I asked, shaken by his words.

'Candles – I'll get candles,' he muttered and went through to the kitchen.

'There's candles and tinder in the dresser in the living-room,' came Mistress Mallett's harsh reply. 'Don't you come worrying. I'll be gone in no time.'

Roger returned, walked past the dresser and sat at the table opposite me.

'She's busy,' he explained. 'There are candles out there and I'll light them from the fire when she's left.'

It was a deliberate lie.

'One candle will be enough,' I replied coldly.

'I don't mind being in the dark,' he said.

No, I thought, so much can be accomplished in the dark with an unwary opponent, but I'm as watchful as you. I wedged my knee under the table so that it could not be tipped unexpectedly.

Roger suddenly leaned across and looked earnestly up into my face.

'You know what you said just now about time, that it devoured everything,' he began. '*Tempus* – something or other –'

' "*Tempus edax rerum*",' I repeated.

'Do you believe that?'

'Of course,' I replied, and the latch clicked as Mallett's wife left the house. 'Look at the ground outside being de-voured by the grass. A few more years and the house itself will become rotten. That's time, devouring, destroying –'

'Only one sort of time,' he interrupted impatiently. 'I mean another sort – a – a time that is only a cover, that we have to live by in hours and minutes, which doesn't really exist. I'm hopeless at expressing myself.' He sounded desperate. 'You must understand – now listen. Something like it comes in a piece of poetry – you won't have heard it, but it doesn't matter:

> "In every land thy feet may tread
> Time like a veil is round thy head;
> Only the land thou seek'st with me
> Never hath been nor yet shall be."

Don't you believe that time is only a veil and if you lift it, you can be anywhere at any period of existence?' he whispered. ' "Time, like a veil is round thy head".'

The words dropped into the hollow stillness of the empty house and became one with the little ghosts crying aloud from another world.

A flicker of light beyond the hedge in the outer darkness shook me from my stupor. My hand flew to my sword.

'That's Mallett with half the village at his heels come to drive the soldier from his stronghold,' I exclaimed in rising anger, springing to my feet.

Roger leapt up too.

'A siege – a siege!' he shouted joyfully. 'Let's barricade the house and pour buckets of boiling oil on their heads like they do in history.'

He was no accomplice, of that I was sure – but what he was I had not the courage to admit. I ignored his flippancy.

'No fighting – yet,' I commanded. 'I've come in peace and I'll try to speak to them first. You fasten the gate by the terrace and then meet me at the stables – but don't be foolhardy. They may fire.'

'With one of those carbines?' he scoffed, dashing from the room. 'Wouldn't hit a cow at five yards. Oh, for a Winchester and I'd pick 'em off like flies.'

I wiped my hands, damp with the fear of some unknown power, not the fear of Mallett's Clubmen.

I was the first to be fired upon. As I stepped from the kitchen into the black night a shot shattered the window
behind me.

'Mallett!' I shouted, groping blindly. 'Enough. I want
peace.'

The light from an unshuttered lantern stabbed the darkness. It shone on the barrel of a carbine and on the leaping
figure of Roger as he whooped towards it.

'Don't fire!' I yelled.

Too late Mallett struck the gun from the man's hands. The
shot rang out and Roger was poised a pace from the smoking
barrel's mouth.

He did not move as I approached. There was a faint smile
on his lips and his eyes wore an odd distant look.

'That must be like the silver bullet in the fairy stories that's
supposed to kill the devil,' he said quietly. 'It doesn't really
kill him. It just gets rid of him for a while.'

'You're hurt,' I said, slipping an arm round his shoulders.

At the edge of the grass I laid his already drooping form on
my coat. Then kneeling at his side I fumbled with the worn
cloth of his doublet, feeling through his shirt to his chest.

'There's no blood – no wound,' I whispered.

'There won't be,' he murmured. 'I'm not going to die yet.
I shall be alive long after you are dead – more than three
hundred years.'

I gazed into that still face which glimmered among the
grasses like a white moth at rest.

He raised one hand to touch my hair, my cheek, my linen
shirt, the hilt of my sword.

'Captain John Knapton,' and I sensed he was smiling. 'I've
always wanted to know what you were really like. Now I
know you were a Roundhead soldier as well while everyone
else just believes you to be the man who laid out the gardens.'

'Gardens?' I asked softly.

'Gardens here – that everyone comes to see, and pays to see,' he chuckled. 'The sundial on the terrace with your name and words in English round the rim. Wonder why you did that? Most people would have used Latin.' He stirred restlessly. 'It's so short a time, so short, and there was so much I wanted to see, to ask – and I thought I could be here for ever if I wanted. The suit was in the chest – I found it there, all folded and old just as he had put it away. And then I hoped I might meet you. I frightened him, old Edward Knapton, and the villagers were half scared – it was too soon and I pestered the life out of him asking what he was doing in your house for everyone knew it was your house. They hadn't a clue it belonged to him first – they even thought you built it.'

His fingers slipped from my sword and lay, a featherweight, on my own.

'He was afraid of me,' he murmured. 'I was something out of this world to him, I suppose.'

I heard the wind bending the limes, the leaves tapping the flags, but the voices were stilled. There was only peace in the clouded night.

The supernatural is to be feared – and I was no longer afraid.

I watched him, how long I watched him, I cannot tell. His slight form a shadow in the flattened grass until, as the moonless hours crept by, he drifted like a moth into the darkness.

My coat was warm when I took it up and stumbled into the house. I lit a candle with the tinder that I now believed Roger had not known how to use and climbed to my uncle's room. There I opened the chest and there I found the blue-grey doublet and breeches, lace shirt, fresh-folded in lavender, as my uncle had put them away only a few months ago. The dust and creases, the yellowing of age and faded colours that

Roger had worn, would come with the years, three hundred years of time.

I knelt there, my head bowed in my arms. I, who had never allowed myself to feel the need for a home, now wanted this my inheritance, though willed to me in fear – and wanted to create out of its wilderness something living, to take the place of the destruction which had been five years of my life.

Was it possible to raise a memorial to a ghost from the future, to a boy not yet born, a memorial that would endure until he came?

It was, for Roger had said so. Oaks and almost everlasting yews, stone seats, slips from each plant to replace the parent as it died, warmth, colour and green lawns. And on the terrace, the sundial – no Latin maxim for a boy who knew no Latin tongue –

'Long looked for – come at last,' I breathed to the sputtering candle, for come at last he would, though in my lifetime I should look for him in vain.

I went to the window and gazed across the dim grasses in the early dawn, already seeing in my mind the garden that was to be. The countryside lay deserted, contented – from Mallett I knew I had no more to fear.

I've lived three centuries in half a day, I thought.

'Be quick, be quick, be quick,' sang a thrush from the limes.

Smiling, I took Dodds' keys from my pocket and tossed them in my palm.

'I'll be quick,' I said. 'And now there is no need to return these – for Master Ghost and I have become well acquainted.'

TSERING TOPYGAL

A TRUE STORY FROM TIBET

TSERING TOPYGAL was twelve years old when he fled from Tibet into India. He became ill and the doctors said he would die within the next few months unless he had a heart operation. This was impossible in India.

The Save the Children Fund members in Australia and New Zealand rallied around, and in a few weeks, Tsetop, as he was called, accompanied by a young Tibetan interpreter, stepped off the plane at Auckland airport wearing his traditional costume and clutching a box marked 'X-Rays' from which he would not be parted.

Just before his operation he revealed that the box contained twenty drawings done by himself and other Tibetan children, which he hoped to be able to sell to pay for his operation.

The Auckland branch of The Save the Children Fund arranged for the drawings to be auctioned and they fetched £530. But the surgeon refused to take his fee for performing the operation, which took five hours, and the hospital insisted that Tsetop was their guest.

So when he returned well again, to the Save the Children emergency camp which was his home, he asked that the money should be kept and used for some other child who needed the same sort of help.

In 1959 thousands of Tibetan children fled from their country and followed their leader, the Dalai Lama, into exile. At the request of the Dalai Lama, The Save the Children Fund opened emergency homes and camps in Northern India for the children. Today, in Simla, the Fund provides complete care and education for nearly 100 Tibetan children.

NOEL STREATFEILD

The Sampler

BENTLEY was a smart neighbourhood. Once it had been a small village called Little Bentley but promoters had bought up the whole place and had turned it into what they advertised as 'exclusive gentlemen's residences with every modern amenity'. All that was left of Little Bentley was the church, which was Norman, and one cottage.

Old Ben, who had been a hedger and ditcher in the days of Little Bentley, said it had been a pretty village.

'Nice green there was wi' a pond and ducks swimming on it. When I was a lad of a May morning I paid a penny on the green to see the May Queen.'

Old Ben, when he was so minded, came over and did a bit of gardening for Mrs Court who lived in the cottage. It was not supposed that Mrs Court was able to pay old Ben for she was known to be very poor. But old Ben did not seem to mind. He firmly refused all offers from the rich householders to do gardening for them saying:

'I known Mrs Court to touch me cap to since I were a tiddler and she lived in the Manor House. She and me know what's what, which nobody else don't hereabouts.'

With Mrs Court lived Annie Boas, her maid, who was believed to be nearly as old as she was, and her great-granddaughter Lavinia, who was ten. Mrs Court had given a home to Lavinia since she was a baby when an accident had deprived her of both parents.

Locally Lavinia was an object of pity. While the other children drove in their rich cars to expensive day or boarding schools she travelled by bus to the Junior Mixed in the nearest town.

'I know the Courts owned the Manor House once,' the Mums in the rich houses would say to each other, 'but that must have been hundreds of years ago. Anyway I'm not asking Lavinia to my party. It wouldn't be kind for the poor child has nothing to wear.'

There was still a Manor House but it had been so modernized it is doubtful if Mrs Court would have recognized it, had she been able to see it. In it now lived Charles Harris, his wife Violet and his two children, Simon and Lucy. Mr Harris was so rich he made all the other rich men living in the neighbourhood feel poor. He was so rich that he was always mentioned in the national papers when they were writing about money. But he was generous, for he gave vast sums to build wings on to hospitals and he was always ready to help when help was needed.

Charles Harris was too, according to his lights, a splendid parent. There was nothing from a pony to a miniature car racing track he did not give his children. As the richest man in the neighbourhood he expected them to lead in whatever was going on. He begged them to get up gymkhanas, to take a car load of children to London for the day and to give fabulous parties. Unfortunately for him Simon and Lucy were quiet children who loathed putting themselves forward. They shuddered at the thought of organizing anything and they hated best clothes and parties. They had in fact only one real friend and she was, to their mother's dismay, Lavinia.

'I do wish you'd tell them they mustn't know her,' Violet would complain to Charles. 'There are such nice children round about they could make friends with, then why pick on that child? I'm not sure she's even clean.'

This was not true. It was true that the cottage was dusty and cobwebby because old Annie could no longer see very well and was too old for much cleaning, but Lavinia, though her clothes were old-fashioned and shabby, was clean, for she was a competent child and could look after herself.

But Charles Harris refused to interfere.

'There's no crime in being poor,' was all he would say.

Simon and Lucy were charmed by Mrs Court's cottage and everything in it. Mrs Court was bed-ridden but sometimes as a treat they were taken up to call on her. Then she would talk about the old days when she lived in the Manor House. The pity was that she rambled rather, for the children were fascinated by what she told them.

'Six horses in the stables – our coachman was called Boas, Annie is his niece – we had a tiger – that's what we called the boy who held the horses, young Robert he was – Mama drove out calling every afternoon – the servants used to stand outside the church to make their bobs to the family as we came out. ...' Then suddenly the old lady would drift away, whispering a string of names which meant nothing.

But Simon and Lucy were not only dependent on Lavinia's great-grandmother for a description of how the house had looked, for there was the sampler.

The sampler in a frame hung above the cottage parlour over-mantel. It was a cross-stitch sampler worked in silk thread on coarse linen. Round the edge there was a border. At the top there was the alphabet. Then there was the picture of a house. It was the manor as it must have been when Mrs Court was a little girl and had worked the sampler. It was impossible to recognize the Manor House for in the days when the sampler had been worked there had been no swimming pool or landscape garden and no rebuilding. Instead the cross-stitch picture showed a lovely house surrounded by a green lawn, and in the foreground were closed wrought iron gates. Under the picture of the house Great-grandmother had worked: 'Except the Lord build the house: their labour is but lost that build it. Except the Lord keep the city: the watchman waketh but in vain.'

'That's a psalm,' Lavinia told Simon and Lucy. 'Great-grandmother had to learn a psalm every Sunday.'

Under the psalm were worked three birds and three trees. At the bottom was Great-grandmother's name. She too was Lavinia. 'Lavinia Court her work finished December 1882 in her ninth year.'

It seemed impossible to the children that they had actually talked to somebody who was nine in 1882. Yet there, huddled in shawls in her bed, was that same Lavinia who had made the sampler in her ninth year.

Simon and Lucy knew the sampler was very important to Lavinia. This worried them because they had learned that nothing in Mrs Court's cottage was safe. Only too often Lavinia would say things like, 'There used to be a lovely table here but it had to be sold,' or, 'We had a clock that chimed, you could change the chime, but that was sold when I was six.'

There seemed to be almost no regular money coming into the cottage; nothing, Simon and Lucy learned, not even the beds, was safe. Without warning, when there was again no money, Lavinia would be told to start for school early in order to leave a note for old Ben, who now lived in the town in a council flat. The note would mean an antique dealer whom Ben knew would come to the cottage and buy whatever it was Great-grandmother would sell. He would take whatever it was away in his van and then for a time there was money.

'But we have very little left to sell,' Lavinia would say. 'Most of the furniture we have now is no good, it was poor stuff Great-grandmother never used.'

Then one day Simon asked outright.

'Do you suppose she would sell the sampler?'

The change in Lavinia was frightening. She turned a sort of greenish yellow and her eyes had a staring look. Her voice seemed to fade so that she could only speak in a whisper.

'That's what I'm scared of. The only hope is that it wouldn't bring in much money. I saw a sampler in a window once, it was more faded than ours and I went in and asked what it cost and the man said £3 10s.'

Walking home Simon said to Lucy:

'Why do you suppose Lavinia gets in such a state about that old sampler? She doesn't seem to mind when other things are sold.'

They were just outside their own gates. Lucy stopped there.

'I think there's a secret thing she isn't telling us.'

'What sort of thing?' Simon asked.

'I don't know but I mean to find out.'

Three days later Simon and Lucy were being driven back from school by Hobbs, the chauffeur. Hobbs had to collect some parcels so he had left the children in the car. It was then that they saw Lavinia. She was hurrying along the street looking terribly pale and tears were pouring down her cheeks. In her arms was a squarish brown paper parcel.

'My goodness, I bet that's the sampler!' said Simon. 'I bet it is.'

They got out of the car and ran to Lavinia.

'Have you got to sell it?' Lucy asked.

Lavinia nodded for she couldn't speak. At last she whispered: 'I'm to take it to the antique man in this street. I'm to try and get five pounds.'

Lucy was nearly crying too.

'Oh Lavinia. How awful! Couldn't you say the man wouldn't buy it?'

But Simon saw an answer.

'Get into the car, Lavinia. Between us Lucy and I have got more than five pounds in our money-boxes. We'll buy the sampler for you. You can take it home.'

Lavinia shook her head and with a struggle found her voice.

'It would be no good. I couldn't take it home again and I've nowhere to hide it. You see, if I brought it back Annie will tell Great-grandmother and she won't take charity, which it would be because you don't want the sampler.'

'Yes we do,' said Simon. 'Don't we, Lucy? And we'll hang it up where you can come and see it every day.'

A shade more colour came into Lavinia's cheeks.

'Oh! Would you buy it? Would you really? If you would keep it for now I'll pay you back when I'm twelve. I'll get a paper round or something, lots of the sisters of the girls at my school do that.'

Hobbs looked disapprovingly at Lavinia when he saw her sitting between Simon and Lucy in the car, for it was well known in the house that Mrs Harris did not approve of her as a friend for the children. And in the house what Mrs Harris thought was what mattered for Charles Harris was away all day. Hobbs was still more disapproving when he discovered he was not dropping Lavinia at the cottage but driving her to the Manor.

Luckily for the children Mrs Harris had people to tea that afternoon so all three were able to get upstairs to the children's sitting-room without being seen.

'Tea will just be coming,' said Simon, 'but first we'll get your money.'

Lavinia had not been inside the Manor House before. She had only been in the garden, for since she was disapproved of it was easier for the children after they had finished their tea to visit her in the cottage. If Lavinia had not been so upset this would have been an occasion and even as it was, while Simon and Lucy were out of the room, she looked in amazement at what had been their nursery and was now their sitting-room. Such luxury! The room looked as if it was out of a shop window. Their tea when it came was beyond Lavinia's imagination. Did they have tea like that every day or was it special for her? Four kinds of sandwiches, four plates of cakes and biscuits and a large cutting cake.

It was after tea when the moment came to hang up the sampler that Lavinia became strange.

'You couldn't hang it in here,' she said firmly. 'It will feel odd – I mean it wouldn't...' and then she broke off.

'Wouldn't what?' Lucy asked.

Simon gave her a nudge.

'Where shall we hang it then?'

Lavinia sounded worried.

'I don't know yet. Can I look?'

'Course you can,' said Simon. 'There's no hurry.'

In the end Lavinia chose a place to hang the sampler. It was at the end of a passage where there was a bare wall.

'It will be all right here. I can feel it will like it.'

That wasn't the end. Lavinia fussed about the position of the nail which Simon wanted to hammer into the wall.

'The sampler must be low enough to look straight into,' she explained.

'But it was over the mantelshelf in your cottage,' said Lucy.

Lavinia nodded.

'I know but I stood on a chair.'

Lucy stared at her feeling fuller and fuller of curiosity.

'There's a secret about that sampler, isn't there?'

Lavinia turned and faced the other two.

'Yes. But it's only to do with me. If it was to do with you I'd tell you because you've bought it.'

'Even if it's got nothing to do with us we'd like to know,' Lucy pleaded. 'Please tell us.'

'Please do,' Simon added.

Lavinia turned back to the sampler. She seemed lost for a minute while she stared at it. At last she said:

'There's a way in. I've been lots of times.'

Simon and Lucy gasped.

'Do you mean into the sampler?' Simon asked.

'Not the sampler, into the garden.' Lavinia put a finger on the gates. 'I go through those and up the drive.'

Lucy said:

'Inside is the garden like it is now or like in the sampler?'

Lavinia sounded far away.

'I don't know. I never go farther than just inside the gates. I could I think but I haven't tried.'

'Why haven't you tried?' Simon asked.

'Because if I went in I might not want to come back.' Lavinia turned again to face them. 'You just can't think how awful it is at Great-grandmother's. There's never enough to eat and in the winter hardly any fires except when Ben cuts up some wood. I wear these awful clothes and they laugh at me at school but there' – she swung back to the sampler –

'everything will be perfect, I know it will, so when I go inside I shall stay.'

'Why don't you go now if you so much want to?' Simon asked.

'I'm waiting until my Great-grandmother dies. You see, I can help a bit to make her happy. I pick her flowers and I do shopping in the town.'

'What I don't see,' said Simon, 'is why only you can go in. Why can't Lucy and I?'

Somewhere a clock struck six.

'I must go,' said Lavinia. But she hesitated. 'It's something I've got which lets me in.'

Lucy was skipping with eagerness to know.

'What is it? Do tell us.'

'It's a needle. One my Great-grandmother used when she was embroidering the sampler. When I press the needle against the gates they just open.'

'Lavinia,' said Simon, 'come to tea tomorrow and bring the needle. Please do. I bet if you can open the gate there's some way in which Lucy and I can creep in behind you. Do let us try.'

Lavinia was very conscious of the five pounds the children had paid for the sampler.

'I'll bring the needle,' she agreed. 'But I don't think it will work. I think it only does for me.'

The next day Lavinia came to tea and she had the needle stuck into a piece of flannel in her pocket. But though she tried to open the gate nothing happened. The truth was it was an awkward sort of day. Simon and Lucy's mother had seen Lavinia arrive and, though she had said nothing except a rather snubbing 'good afternoon,' all three children were conscious she was in the house and might come up at any moment.

Back in the sitting-room Lavinia said:

'I'm sorry. Sometimes it doesn't work, today is one of those days.'

'Come again tomorrow,' Lucy begged. 'Perhaps it will work then.'

Lavinia shook her head.

'Let's wait for a day when you know your mother is out. It's always a slow thing getting in and I can't do it if I feel someone might interrupt.'

It was ten days before the right day arrived. Then Simon and Lucy were waiting for Lavinia at the bus stop. Lucy clutched at Lavinia's arm.

'Mum and Dad have gone to London for a dinner. Today's the day. We've got ages and no one will interrupt.'

'Can we get the needle?' Simon asked.

Nobody seemed to care what happened to Lavinia. She slipped into the cottage and in two minutes was out again with the precious needle.

'I shouted to Annie I was going out to tea but I don't think she noticed.'

The children ran all the way to the Manor House. In the sitting-room they gobbled their tea then they hurried into the passage. The sun through a window was shining on the sampler.

'The house in the picture looks much nicer than it looks now,' sighed Lucy.

'I've thought of a way it might work,' said Lavinia. 'Put your arms round my waist, Lucy, and you put yours round hers, Simon, and when I say "Now" push.'

The children did as she told them and Lavinia held out the needle.

'It doesn't happen quickly. I have to look and look until it goes fuzzy, then I press with the needle and then sometimes the gates open.'

Lucy, scarcely daring to breathe, clung to Lavinia, and

Simon to Lucy. It seemed that ages passed then Lavinia's voice, full of excitement, called out:

'Now.'

They were through. It was a sunny day. The grass was spangled with daisies. On a grey wall a wisteria was swinging in the breeze. Then the children began to hear sounds: a cuckoo singing, a dog barking. Then something happened which startled Lavinia for it had never happened before.

A carriage pulled by two horses came trotting round from the back of the house to the front door. It was driven by a very smart coachman wearing a top hat with a sort of little windmill on the side of it. Sitting beside him was a boy in the same uniform. The boy jumped down and went to the horses' heads to hold them. Then the front door was opened by a butler and out came a lady. A very smart lady dressed in grey silk with a silk shawl and a pretty linen bonnet with flowers on it. She was helped by the butler into the carriage. Then the butler said to the boy holding the horses: 'Ready, Robert.' The boy jumped up to his seat beside the coachman and the carriage came trotting down the drive towards the children. When it reached them the lady called out 'Stop,' and she leant out and she spoke to Lavinia.

'My dearest child, what are you doing? You should be at your needlework. What children are these?'

'These are Simon and Lucy,' Lavinia explained.

The lady looked displeased.

'Run along home, children, you know you should not be playing with Miss Lavinia. Your mother is a good woman and knows her place and she should teach you yours.'

Dismayed, Lavinia looked at Simon and Lucy. Where was home? It had never crossed her mind when she had opened the gate that they might be separated. But now, looking first at herself and then at Simon and Lucy, she could see that they didn't seem the sort of children the lady in the carriage would think suitable friends for her. For while she was dressed in a blue silk frock they were very poorly dressed and they had no shoes or stockings.

'Run along, children,' the lady said sharply.

Not knowing what else to do Simon and Lucy hurried to the gate and ran, but not back into their own passage as they had expected, but out on to a village green with a pond with ducks swimming on it.

'Where do you suppose home is?' Lucy whispered to Simon.

'Someone will tell us,' Simon said, sounding braver than he felt. 'Anyway Lavinia has the needle, we can go back whenever we like.'

At that moment a cottage door opened and a woman came to the gate, she was poorly dressed in a shabby black dress which swept the ground but she was wearing a clean white apron. She spoke with so strong an accent Simon and Lucy found her hard to understand.

'There you are! Get the pails, Simon, and fetch the water. There's the washing to be hung, Lucy. Be careful wi' the pegs, there was a complaint about a mark on one of little Miss Lavinia's muslins.'

Back at the Manor Lavinia found herself walking, as if she knew the way, through the front door and into the house. It looked very different inside from the way it looked as the Harrises had it. For one thing it was very dark, and made darker by crimson satin curtains. Somebody seemed fond of shooting animals for there were heads of enormous beasts hung on both sides of the hall, and at the bottom of the stairs there was a whole lion skin and head. There was too rather a museum look for on dark marble pillars there were busts of what Lavinia guessed were distinguished old relations.

Without knowing why she climbed up the red-carpeted stairs to the top of the house. There she opened a little white gate and found herself in what were evidently nurseries.

'Really!' she thought. 'A nursery at my age! For I bet I'm at least nine. But perhaps there are younger children.'

There were. A little boy who looked about six but it was hard to judge for he was so oddly dressed in green velvet with a lace collar. As well there was a baby in a cradle.

In charge were a nurse and a nursemaid. Both wore print dresses down to the ground, white aprons, and on their heads were caps. The cap looked funny on the nursemaid, who did not look much older than Lavinia, and evidently was not used to having her hair up, still less pinning a cap on it.

The little boy flung himself at Lavinia.

'Will you play with me, Vinnie? Will you play trains?'

'Now, Master Horace,' said Nurse. 'Miss Lavinia has no time to play now. She has to get on with her sampler. Annie looked in just now on Miss Crabbe, she was sleeping so she didn't disturb her. Take off your boots, dear, and put on your slippers, then go down to the schoolroom and get on with your needling.'

That was the first time Lavinia realized she was wearing boots. Imagine boots and black stockings! While changing into her slippers Lavinia had a closer look at herself. Her blue frock buttoned all down the back and finished in a bow at the bottom of her spine. Underneath she wore the most extraordinary amount of under garments. A fine white petticoat trimmed with lace. A plain white petticoat, a scalloped flannel petticoat and what she had been told used to be called drawers. These were to her knees and, like the petticoat, were trimmed with lace.

Her schoolroom when she found it was the room the Harrises used as the children's sitting-room. But oh, how different it looked! No gay paint or curtains, instead heavy curtains of green velvet, stiff chairs on which you had to sit upright, and a plain schoolroom table with a globe on it. In the window on a frame was the sampler. It was, Lavinia noticed, nearly finished. So I must be nine, she thought, and I must be Great-grandmother. How very odd!

It did not take Lavinia long to step into her Great-grandmother's shoes for everything seemed to happen at the same time every day. In the mornings she did lessons with Miss Crabbe. In the afternoons she either took a walk round the village with Miss Crabbe or she went driving with her Mama. After tea she went upstairs to be helped by Annie to change. This was an elaborate affair for everything came off, even the underclothes, for in the evenings her top petticoat and her drawers were edged with real lace. Frocks for the evening were white silk with a frill round the bottom and tied with a wide soft silk sash of pink or blue.

Annie puzzled Lavinia at first because she reminded her

of someone. Then one day Annie, who was a chatterbox, telling a story said: 'And cook she said to me, if that's the way you carry a tray, Annie Boas, you'll never rise to be an upper servant.'

So that was it! This was Annie Boas and no wonder she seemed old in the cottage for she was now twelve, so that meant she was three years older than Great-grandmother.

What Lavinia liked best was not the good food or the quiet orderly household, it was the love everybody gave her. Horace, dressed in black velvet with a real lace collar, would squeeze her hand as they walked downstairs after tea and whisper 'Oh Vinnie, I do love you.' Her mother would kiss her and hug her and call her 'my own darling child', and every night both Papa and Mama would come up to kiss her goodnight. Nurse and all the servants called her 'Miss Lavinia dear' and she even got fond of poor shabby little Miss Crabbe, who was always patting her hand and saying 'What a dear child you are growing up to be.' 'Almost she sounds surprised,' Lavinia thought, 'as if Great-grandmother was more difficult than me. But I suppose she was for she was born to all this instead of coming to it suddenly after having nothing, like me.'

But there was worry as well as happiness. It was so terribly difficult to talk to Simon and Lucy, for to be seen talking to them was considered naughty. Mama and Papa, Miss Crabbe, Nurse and all the servants from the butler downwards were great believers in 'knowing your place'. Never once was Lavinia able to visit them in their cottage – indeed the only times she could see them was when they brought back or fetched the washing their mother laundered. This happened twice a week, it was collected on Mondays and brought back on Saturdays. Always Lavinia managed to be about when they came, which was luckily early before she started lessons, and always she saved food for them. Oh dear, how miserable Simon and Lucy were! Lucy was nearly always crying.

'You can't think how awful it is, Lavinia. Nothing to eat except bread and milk and vegetables, we're always hungry for we only have meat once a week.'

'We don't go to school,' Simon complained, 'so we work all day long. I have to carry meat for the butcher and it weighs a ton, and that's only the half of it.'

'I have to scare birds,' Lucy sobbed, 'and it's awful when there are stones and nettles for we've no shoes.'

'And when we get home,' Simon added, 'it's "fetch this, carry that". It's not our mother's fault for the man who would have been our Dad is dead and widows don't get pensions this side of the sampler.'

'Oh please, please, Lavinia, do get us back,' Lucy pleaded.

'Or lend us the needle and let us try on our own,' Simon suggested.

Lucy gave another sob.

'However awful it was for you living with your Great-grandmother it was never as bad as it is for us living where we are now. It isn't only we're always hungry but the butcher beats Simon.'

Lavinia was terribly sorry but she did so dreadfully want to stay so she played for time.

'It's no good lending you the needle for you couldn't get through alone, I know you couldn't. Give me a little longer and then I'll get you back.'

'Well please, please be quick,' Lucy would plead. 'Honestly we can't bear it. Poor children have a dreadful time this side of the sampler.'

Then something happened which made Lavinia feel she could never go back. Horace, who was having riding lessons, had a bad fall. He injured his spine. The doctor was very worried about him and sent for specialists all the way from

London. But they shook their heads and it was clear they were afraid Horace would never walk again. Lavinia was heartbroken because she could remember a little water colour of Great-grandmother's. It was of a small boy in a green velvet suit with a lace collar and Great-grandmother saying: 'That was my little brother Horace, he never lived to grow up.' Was this accident the beginning of the end for Horace? Every second when she was not otherwise employed Lavinia spent playing with him, and she knew, for everybody said so, when she was not there that he lay with his eyes on the door waiting for her to come.

'Oh Lavinia!' Mama would say. 'What should I do without you? You have no idea what a comfort you are to your Papa and myself.'

One day when Lavinia was playing with Horace Annie came into the room.

'Could I speak to you, Miss Lavinia?'

Lavinia got up.

'I shall only be a few minutes, Horace.'

Annie drew Lavinia into the passage.

'It's the widow's children from the cottage. Crying and carrying on terrible little Lucy is. She says she must speak to you.'

Lavinia's heart sank.

'Where are they?'

'Well, as none of the gardeners were about and Miss Crabbe is resting and your Mama out driving I've put them in the summerhouse.'

Lavinia ran down the garden. Simon and Lucy were in such a state they could hardly speak.

'It's come to the point when our mother just can't go on any more,' Lucy wailed.

'She said she was sad to do it but it was the only way she knew,' Simon added.

'The last boy he had died,' Lucy sobbed.

'What boy? Who had?' Lavinia asked.

Simon pulled himself together.

'I'm being sold to a sweep. It's had to be done in secret because there are laws about boys going up chimneys but it's going to happen. The sweep is coming for me tonight.'

Lavinia was appalled. She had read *The Water Babies* and remembered what happened to poor Tom.

'Oh no! You mustn't go with him.'

'There is only one way by which I can get out of it,' Simon pointed out. 'I must go back home.'

Lavinia felt torn in half. Upstairs Horace was waiting. Soon dear Mama would come back from her call paying. All her heart was this side of the sampler. But a chimney sweep!

Lucy clutched Lavinia's hands.

'Dear Lavinia, please. If you'll just get us back, you needn't stay you can come through again right away.'

Lavinia was wearing a frock sprigged with pink flowers, it had a pink sash. Never once since she had walked into the sampler had she put the needle where she could not reach it. Now she pulled down a pleat in her sash and pulled out the needle, which was threaded through the silk.

'Come on,' she said. 'We'll go back as we came. You holding on to me, Lucy, and you, Simon, hold on to Lucy.'

It was much more difficult to go back. For a time the gate refused to open when the needle pressed it. As well it seemed as though a strong wind was blowing them backwards. Then there was a loud crack, the gate opened and all three children found themselves sprawled on the floor under the sampler.

Simon was the first to get his breath.

'We're through,' he gasped. 'It's a miracle but we're through.'

A maid passed along the end of the passage. She called out:

'Have you finished your tea? I've come for the tray.'

Simon and Lucy looked at each other. Then they jumped up.

'Tea !' Lucy almost screamed. 'It must be still on the table. Come on, Simon.'

Simon was already half-way down the passage.

'Food ! Glorious food ! Come on, Lavinia.'

But Lavinia did not come on. Instead she searched the floor and soon found what she was looking for. It was what, having heard that loud crack, she had dreaded she would find. The needle was broken into several pieces.

Lavinia stood up and looked at the tapestry. There was the house and all that she loved, but she knew the broken needle would never open the gate. Quietly she slipped out of the house and, seeing badly because her eyes were blinded with tears, she ran home to the cottage.

LITTLE MOTHER

A TRUE STORY FROM UGANDA

THE nurse at The Save the Children Fund Welfare Centre found an eleven-year-old girl nursing a tiny, very frail baby at the end of a queue of mothers. Her name was Kisembo and she explained that her mother had died a week ago and as the baby would not drink the soup she had prepared for it and never stopped crying, she had walked fifteen miles to the clinic with the baby on her back.

Nurse said that the baby ought to go to hospital and Kisembo insisted on going with it. She watched, wide-eyed and attentive as the baby was cared for and fed, and asked many questions. Nurse asked her about school. One could not attend school with a baby to care for, Kisembo explained. And anyway, she wanted to stay at the hospital and learn to be a nurse. There were many, many sick babies in their village who needed caring for.

At last they persuaded her that if she wanted to become a nurse she must first go to school. If she went every day she could come back and stay at the hospital. There were so many things she could do to help; and she would be with her baby.

Kisembo is happy. She learns at school; she learns at the hospital. One day, she says, when her baby is off her hands and she is really trained she will come back to the clinic and take charge. The Doctor and Nurse have no doubt about that.

The Hospital and the nurse and the school Kisembo went to were made possible by The Save the Children Fund. (You helped them by buying this book.)

JOHN ROWE TOWNSEND

The Friday Miracle

A T twenty past three the mothers started arriving at the
school. The school was a private one. It was a big old house
in a wide old street in a pleasant, gently decaying part of the
city.

The mothers arrived in their Minis and Vivas and little
Fiats. They got out of their cars and stood around on the
pavement, chatting till the children appeared. Willis didn't
chat with the mothers. Willis was aloof. Willis drew up at
the other side of the street and sat in the Daimler, motion-
less.

At half past three school ended and out came the children. Some of the smallest ran straight to their mothers' arms. Some sauntered out in twos and threes, joking and laughing. Some fought and shouted and whizzed round in circles, letting off steam.

Ronald and Avril and Ben always walked out sedately, side by side. They looked both ways and crossed the road to Willis and got in the car. Avril thought Willis ought to open the door for them, but he didn't, except on Fridays.

Ben was only seven, and sometimes he boasted at school about Willis and the Daimler.

'We have a chauffeur and a big grey Daimler and another big car at home,' he'd say, 'and my father has a Jaguar, and once he came to meet us in it.'

But the children in his class didn't care.

'My father drives a car transporter,' Simon Malory had answered once, but everyone knew that wasn't true.

Ronald and Avril didn't boast. They were twelve and ten, and they were quiet. They had friends at school but they didn't see them outside, because friendships out of school seemed to start with chats between mothers on the pavement, and arrangements for lifts, and casual invitations to tea. Friendships out of school didn't go with Willis and the Daimler.

Ronald and Avril walked quietly each day to the car with Ben between them. They held one of Ben's hands each, to keep him safe and in order. They walked out of school as they walked into school – not really looking forward to the hours ahead, but ready to put up with them because putting up with them was all you could do.

Except on Fridays, and today was Friday.

On Fridays they ran across the road (just remembering to look both ways and to keep hold of Ben's hands). On Fridays Barbara came and sometimes Father, and Willis opened the door for them. Friday was the day they went to Granny Taylor's. There was no day like Friday.

Today they tumbled into the car, and Willis shut the door and went round to the driver's seat and the car drew away from the kerb. Willis didn't say a word. Willis knew the routine.

It was a pity, thought Ronald and Avril, that Father wasn't there. But Father didn't often come these days. They'd almost given up expecting him.

Ben was excited, as he always was on Fridays.

'Will Heinz Dog be there?' he asked. 'Will the Thorpes be at home? Can Stan and Alice help me make a den in the back yard? What will we have for tea?'

'How should I know, Ben?' Barbara said. Barbara was Father's second wife.

'How should Barbara know?' said Avril, echoing her. 'We don't know till we get there, do we?'

It took twenty minutes to get to Granny Taylor's. Granny Taylor's was a fair-sized, solid red-brick terrace house, one of six. It had a lion knocker on the front door, and if Granny wasn't there to meet them in the doorway Ben always rushed to the knocker and beat a great rat-tat on it.

Today Ben rat-tatted but Granny Taylor didn't come as quickly as usual. Ronald and Avril stood behind Ben. Willis didn't wait. Willis handed two or three parcels out and said 'Six-thirty then, ma'am,' and in a moment the Daimler was gone.

Ben rat-tatted again.

'That's funny,' Barbara said. 'She knows we always come on Fridays.'

Then at last Granny Taylor opened the door, and there were great huggings and kissings, and it wasn't until they were all in the house that they saw that she was limping.

'What ever have you been doing?' Barbara asked.

'I fell,' said Granny Taylor. She looked guilty.

'You *naughty* old thing,' Barbara said.

'I couldn't help it. It was that dark corner on the cellar stairs. I slipped.'

'And I'm not surprised,' said Barbara. She sounded just as if she was talking to Ben. 'At your age you shouldn't set foot on those cellar stairs. Now let me look. You've got a bandage under that stocking, haven't you? ... Ronald and Avril, you can go outside for a few minutes while I talk to your Granny.'

Ben had gone already. He'd disappeared through the back door in search of Stan and Alice Thorpe and their dog Heinz. Ronald and Avril followed as far as the yard. Barbara's voice came down to them from the kitchen window.

'It seems to be going on all right,' she was saying, 'but it's a wonder it wasn't worse. You might have broken your leg, if not your neck. I can't trust you, darling, can I?'

Ronald pulled a face at Avril.

'Poor old Gran,' he said. 'She's in trouble today.'

Then he pushed open the gate into the next yard. Avril knew he'd be looking for Tom Sutton next door. Tom's father had a workshop and tools, and he didn't mind if Tom and his friends used them. Ronald could never wait to get his hands on those tools.

Avril stayed where she was. She heard Barbara's voice again from the kitchen window. And this time came the shock.

'I'm not going to let you stay here *any* longer,' Barbara was saying to Granny Taylor. 'This time I mean it. I shall tell Jim, it's absolutely *impossible* for you to stay here.'

'But I've lived here forty years, dear,' Granny Taylor said. 'It's my home.'

'Forty years! All the more reason for leaving. It's so old-fashioned and awkward. It's too much for you, you know it is. And it's so shabby.'

'Well, it's big enough, that's true,' said Granny Taylor. 'There's room for all of you here, if you wanted to come.'

Avril moved away from the window because she could hear every word and it felt as if she was eavesdropping. But she couldn't get what had been said out of her mind.

She pushed open the door into the next yard. Ronald was there with Tom Sutton, and they didn't notice her because they were busy making some mysterious object with Tom's father's drill, and all round them were hammers and screwdrivers and planes and pieces of wood and shavings. From two or three doors farther on she could hear the barking of Heinz and the shouts of Ben, playing with Stan and Alice Thorpe. 'There's room for all of you here, if you wanted to come.' If they lived there it would be like a week of Fridays. But it looked more as if Granny Taylor would be leaving than as if they'd be coming here.

Avril wandered back into the house and helped to lay the kitchen table. They were going to have tea. Scrambled eggs on toast and brown bread and butter and jam and fruit salad and chocolate biscuits and cake.

'I can't think how these children ever get up from the table, with the food you give them,' Barbara said to Granny Taylor. 'And they're supposed to have their supper at seven. It throws everything out when they come here.'

'I'm sorry, dear,' Granny Taylor said. Barbara returned to the first subject.

'And this accident happened at the weekend,' she said, 'and you never told us. You could have let us know, couldn't you? After all, Jim is your only son, and the children are your only grandchildren, and you should tell us when a thing like this happens.'

'Jim's so busy,' Granny Taylor said.

'Well, yes, he is busy. A business the size of his, and growing all the time. He gets so tired and worried. There's some kind of special meeting going on now that's worrying him. But he does think about you, you know.'

'I haven't seen him since Easter.'

'He thinks about you a lot. He says he'll come as soon as the present problems are sorted out.'

'There's always something to be done before I see him,' said Granny Taylor.

'There's nothing to stop you coming to see us any time,' Barbara said. 'You know I'll always send Willis round for you.'

'I don't like it in that cold house,' Granny Taylor said.

'It's not a cold house. It has full central heating.'

'Well, it feels cold to me.'

'You're an obstinate old woman,' said Barbara. She patted Granny's arm, as if to say she wasn't really cross. But she did sound cross all the same. 'You're not fit to be on your own.'

Granny Taylor turned off the gas and ladled scrambled egg on to plates.

'Go and call the others,' she said to Avril.

Avril went for the others. Ben broke away at once from what he was doing, ran into the house and sat at the table, waiting. He loved his meals. Ronald didn't come so quickly. He and Tom Sutton had reached a vital stage of their work. But he came soon enough. Barbara was the only person who didn't much care for high tea at Granny Taylor's. She sipped a cup of tea and ate a biscuit.

Afterwards the boys let Avril help them for a while – mostly holding things – and then she joined Ben and the Thorpes, who'd made a house with blankets and a couple of clothes-horses. Then Susan Gough at the end house came out, and she and Avril knocked a tennis-ball about between

them. Then it was half past six and they were brushing themselves down and Willis was waiting with the car. Granny Taylor sighed a little as she kissed them good-bye.

'Well,' said Barbara to Avril as one woman to another, when they were sitting together in the back seat; 'this time she's learned her lesson. I gave her a good talking-to. She realizes now, she'll just have to give the house up.'

'What, Granny leave her home?'

'She's getting to an age when she just can't cope,' Barbara said.

Ronald leaned over.

'Where will she go?' he asked. 'Will she come and stay with us?'

'No, she wouldn't want to. But we can get her into Sunsets. It's very nice there. It's a kind of hotel for elderly people where they get properly looked after. It almost makes me wish I was old. They have rooms of their own, with all their possessions round them. It's expensive, of course, but your father doesn't mind paying. It will be a relief to us to know she's under supervision.'

'But she won't like it,' said Ronald slowly.

'Oh yes, she will when she's used to it. She'll be very happy there.'

'I shan't like it,' said Avril. 'I shan't like it at all.'

Ben had been listening. Suddenly he burst into tears.

'I won't see Heinz Dog any more,' he wailed. 'Or Stan or Alice. We won't be able to play in our den.'

'You don't want a silly old den of blankets,' said Barbara. 'And as for that mongrel, well, I bear it no malice but it really is a revolting creature . . .'

'I love him,' said Ben. 'I love Heinz Dog. And Stan and Alice.' He sobbed and sobbed. 'I don't want to stop going to Granny Taylor's house.'

'Nor do I,' said Ronald.

'No more lovely Fridays,' said Avril. There was a lump in her throat.

'Now don't be silly,' Barbara said. 'You'll still be able to see Granny Taylor. And probably still on Fridays, if that's what you want.'

'But it won't be the same,' said Avril.

'No, it won't,' said Ronald, fiercely. 'Not at all.'

'It'll just be school and home and Father always busy and never anything nice,' said Avril.

Ben burst into fresh wailings. Ronald and Avril bit their lips.

'Oh, my goodness,' said Barbara. 'What next? It isn't the end of the world.'

'It is,' said Avril. She took Ben's and Ronald's hands. 'I wish a miracle would happen,' she said. 'A Friday miracle. If there's a day for miracles, I'm sure it's Friday.'

But it didn't look the time or place for a miracle. Willis drove steadily on, his back stiff and unyielding. Willis didn't know and didn't care what happened in the back of the car. Willis did his job.

The children weren't taking notice of anything when the car turned into their own drive. But Barbara sat up straight and spoke in surprise.

'They're still all there !' she said.

'Who are?'

'The people who came for the special meeting I was telling you about.'

There were half a dozen cars, all biggish, some chauffeur-driven, parked in the drive. Willis slid past them in the Daimler, stopped at the portico, opened the car doors for Barbara and the children, then drove off towards the garage.

Ben's face was still tearful. Barbara bent down and dabbed at it with the corner of her handkerchief.

'Can't have you going in to see your father like that,' she said.

Then the front door opened and the gentlemen who owned the cars came out. They were middle-aged or elderly, well-dressed, solemn. They didn't seem to want to talk. They raised their hats, passed the time of day briefly, and went on to their cars. One of them noticed Ben's tear-stained face, looked at Barbara with sympathy, and said,

'I'm very sorry, Mrs Taylor. No wish of mine that this should happen.' And he followed the others.

Then Father was at the door. He was smiling. He came out and caught them all in his arms – all at once in a bunch.

'Well!' he said. 'It's all over. Finished. Problems solved at one fell swoop.' He released them.

Barbara looked out between the pillars across the acre-and-a-half of lawn to where the last car was just disappearing through the big wrought-iron gates.

'Jim, please explain,' she said.

'We had a business,' Father said. 'Now we haven't. To-morrow I'll be furious at the thought of ten years' wasted work. But today at this moment I just feel free.'

'You mean they've bought you out?' Barbara said.

'Not exactly. International Castings have taken the business over, debts and all. Which is just as well, seeing there's more debts than anything else. We tried to expand too fast and ran into trouble. They know about the debts, of course, but they still want to get their hands on the firm.'

'So you haven't a job,' Barbara said.

'Not just now. But I'm a trained engineer. I'll get a job soon.'

'And you haven't any money?'

'Not a cent.'

'And the cars?'

'They're the firm's cars. They go with the business.'

'And how will we keep this house up?'

'We won't,' Father said. 'Henry Morris of International says he'll take it over, staff and all. He's had his eye on it for years. So you see. No job, no money, no car, no home. No problems.'

'Except where we're going to live,' said Barbara.

Ben's voice piped up.

'Granny Taylor has a house,' he said. 'She says there's room for all of us there.'

'Don't be silly, Ben,' said Barbara, and then, 'You'll have to give me time, Jim. I can't get used to all this in five minutes.'

'Ben's idea's not so silly as all that,' Father said. 'We could stay there a little while, perhaps, if she'd have us.'

'We could look after her,' Avril said.

'We could change schools,' Ronald said, 'and not pay any money any more.'

'Course she'll have us,' said Ben. 'Course she'll have us. Let's go and tell her right away.'

'What we need first is some dinner,' said Father. He thought for a moment and said, 'Well, why shouldn't we go across and see your Granny?' Then he added, 'On the bus, of course.'

Ben loved buses. He jumped up and danced with delight, all by himself. And as he danced he sang,

'We're off to Granny Taylor's on the bus. We're off to Granny Taylor's on the bus.'

Ronald and Avril, Father and Barbara watched him. They all knew life wasn't as simple as it seemed to Ben. They didn't know what would happen to them. But they smiled, all of them smiled.

TONIO'S GIFT

FIVE-year-old Tonio was chosen to be the youngest shepherd in the Nativity play. The children were asked to bring a present for the babe in the manger. Tonio, whose family was very poor, brought his most precious possession, a piece of wood, worn smooth with handling. It was his only toy, which he had kept hidden and played with in secret, otherwise it would have been taken from him and used for firewood. He wept a little as he parted with it.

A visitor, hearing the story of his gift, sent a beautiful red engine to Tonio in place of his piece of wood. Beaming with delight, Tonio tip-toed to the crib and retrieved his piece of wood, leaving the beautiful red engine in its place.

It will be possible to send presents to other boys like Tonio, because you bought this book.

JENIFER WAYNE

Ice on the Line

'THERE'S ice on the line!' he bawled into the wind. 'Mind how you – *look out!*'

The great wave rose; fingers slipped, feet slithered; the whole sea crashed down.

Then darkness.

'Never mind,' said Aunt Bee brightly. 'It'll be summer in Australia. Just think! I wish I was coming with you: this fog and my arthritis don't agree. Now are you sure you've packed your little jar of Marmite?'

'Don't they have fog in Australia?' asked Rachel. She looked dully out of the window at the frosty tussocks of grass in front of Aunt Bee's cottage.

'Oh I don't think so. Mind you, I know the food in these planes is supposed to be wonderful, but you're so used to your Marmite – I remember your mother telling me when you were quite a baby, how you missed it if . . . Oh well, never mind.'

She had seen Rachel stiffen, and she knew why. I'm a silly

old fool, she said to herself. If I'd lost *my* mother in that dreadful way, at that age. . . .

'Never mind'– that's her password, thought Rachel bitterly. Ought to have it written on her grave.

Then she was just as bitterly sorry. Poor Aunt Bee. She had done her best. She had tried to look after them ever since it happened. Had them in this comfortingly thick-walled, tucked-away cottage, where they had once spent a summer holiday . . .

Rachel stopped in mid-thought. That was the trouble: everywhere was 'where they had once' done something. Her father had shut up the house in London; he knew they couldn't bear to stay there. He had whisked Rachel off to a hotel; to friends; even to a caravan for a week; anything to get her away, to start a new life.

But there was no getting away. Reminders cropped up everywhere – sometimes in the most unexpected places. That café in Scotland, for instance, where they had had tea and welsh rarebit one rainy evening, and suddenly Rachel had noticed the blue milk jug with 'Corfe Castle' scratched on its side in white. Exactly like the one she had bought for her mother the year they went to Dorset . . .

After months of moving around, her father had at last accepted Aunt Bee's invitation to the cottage. But this, in a way, was the worst of all.

For one thing, Rachel remembered it in the summer. Raspberries and peas from the garden; her mother shelling them on a kitchen chair in the sun outside the back door. Now it was winter; winter in every possible way.

Aunt Bee had tried to make Christmas nice for them. She had filled Rachel's stocking – in spite of the fact that Rachel herself had refused to hang it up.

'Don't tell me thirteen's too old for a stocking ! I had one until I was twenty, at least.'

'Young people grow up too quickly these days,' said Aunt Esther gloomily. She was Aunt Bee's older sister, and lived with her, but they were not at all alike. Aunt Bee, in spite of her arthritis, was always bright; Aunt Esther almost always gloomy – though she suffered from nothing at all except a corn. She referred to it, in a martyred and melancholy way, as 'My Little Trouble'.

Yet Rachel found, now, that Aunt Bee's brightness was even harder to stand than Aunt Esther's gloom. So when Aunt Bee said, 'Never mind; I don't suppose Santa Claus takes age into account,' Rachel marched out of the room and slammed the door and stayed upstairs in the cold little bedroom for hours. She remembered how in the summer she used to lie listening to the scratch of birds in the roof under that slanting ceiling; and how her mother's head would pop round the door:

'Hey – nobody's up yet: want to come to the farm with me and fetch the milk?'

Rachel lay in the cold and cried; at supper-time she sat over her soup in stony silence, rejected the treacle tart, and said, 'I don't feel like it,' when her great-aunts offered to play a game of cards.

But still Aunt Bee filled her stocking: or rather, filled one of her own thick woollen ones, and crept in at two o'clock on Christmas morning to lay it on the end of the bed.

But it was all no good. Rachel's father tried hard to put on a cheerful face, but by Boxing Day he had decided.

'I've been offered this job,' he told the aunts. 'I suppose it's a godsend, really. She'll never get over it here. Australia: well, at least it'll give her new horizons. Me too,' he added, though he very rarely referred to his own feelings.

'Of course he feels guilty, poor dear,' said Aunt Bee later. 'I can understand it.'

'Meg would insist on going,' said Aunt Esther. 'He didn't want her to.'

'No, but it was his boat.'

'Madness; fishing in the North Sea in a thing like that. It's a miracle they weren't all three of them drowned.'

'She was the active type,' sighed Aunt Bee. 'Adventurous. D'you remember how even as a little girl –'

'Obstinate,' said Aunt Esther.

'No fear at all; I believe she'd have sailed the thing single-handed if she'd had half a chance.'

'These people never stop to think how they endanger others,' Aunt Esther said bitterly. 'Those poor men who had to risk their lives picking them up. . . .' But she was not really bitter at heart; just helpless in the face of disaster. Quite helpless, she knew, to comfort Rachel; the child seemed totally removed from all comfort, let alone anything that could be done by a couple of old spinsters. Aunt Esther was more of a realist than Aunt Bee; she knew that mere brightness was no use, even if she had been capable of it.

'I'm sure I do her more harm than good,' she grunted, and went up to bed with Her Little Trouble encased in its camel-coloured felt bootee.

When the great day came, Aunt Esther announced that she was going up to town for the Sales, trouble or no trouble, fog or no fog. They needed some new sheets and bath towels.

'But you won't be here to see them off!' protested Aunt Bee.

'What good would that do?' said Aunt Esther, and went on the early bus.

'Tell them I wanted to get a train back before the rush-hour!' she called as the stumped off through the frost.

Aunt Bee wondered how she could tell them anything so heartless. Australia was so far away; so final; they might never see them again . . .

But it was Esther who had left the little jar of Marmite. Not that Rachel or her father seemed to notice anything or anyone very much just now. He was preoccupied with checking times of trains and planes and the luggage; Rachel simply stood around and stared out of windows. All Aunt Bee could do was to go on trying to be bright.

At last the taxi came. The driver asked for a jug of hot water.

'Radiator's frozen up,' he said. And then, when he saw the labels on the cases, 'Australia, eh? Lovely. Sunshine and blue skies out there now. I envy you, gettin' away from this lot.' He glanced disgustedly at the foggy common, the icicles on the joints of the cottage water-pipes. 'Like to take me with you?' he grinned at Rachel. She couldn't grin back.

'I keep telling them how lucky they are,' said Aunt Bee rather desperately. 'Mind you send a postcard, dear – and happy journey!'

She kissed Rachel, who simply said, 'You'd better not stand out in the cold.'

'Oh, never mind that,' said Aunt Bee. 'Never mind. . . .'

They were the last words Rachel heard as the taxi moved off.

But Aunt Bee did mind. Back in the cottage by herself, she shivered at the thought of that long journey. She hoped the train wouldn't be too cold; that the fog would have cleared by the time they got to the Airport; that Rachel wouldn't feel sick. Outside, the frost still lay on the garden as stiffly at lunch time as it had at dawn. The dead thistleheads bristled with it; the raspberry canes and peasticks were black as witches' besoms against the rough white earth.

Aunt Bee boiled herself an egg; the cottage seemed very empty, now that all those suitcases had gone out of the hall.

The light, at three o'clock, was already beginning to fade; she hoped Esther would be home soon.

A knock at the door. 'Now who can that be? – Unless Esther's forgotten her key . . .' The two sisters had so few visitors, and were so well-known to all the 'locals' in this place, that formal knocks were rare. The milkman from the farm always whistled; the baker said 'Oi!'; the grocer with the weekly order just walked in.

'I do hope it's Esther. If it is, I'll put the kettle on and we'll have another –' But as soon as she had opened the door two inches, she stopped.

A strange man! I ought to have put the chain up, she thought, and said quickly, 'Not today, thank you.' One heard of such awful things.

But the man said, just as quickly, 'Mr Snowdon – is he

here? Mr John Snowdon, he used to own a boat called *The Gannet*, I was his crew, we were told he might have come here, him and the little girl.' He sounded as if he was holding back some great hope.

' "We"?'

Aunt Bee peered out; there was a car by the gate, and two huddled figures in it. They were so camouflaged by coats and scarves and rugs that you couldn't tell if they were men or women.

But the man at the door – yes, she recognized him now. She had seen a snapshot of him, with Rachel's father, standing on the deck of that lost boat. Bob, his name was; Bob, or Bill....

'Yes, they were here,' she said, 'but you've missed them. They went this morning.'

'Went?' His face turned blank with disappointment. 'Where did they go? Where can I find them? It's very important.'

'You can't. They've gone to Australia.'

'Australia !' This time he turned really pale. 'Australia. I don't believe it. After all this time – and now today ! Today, you said.' He looked so dazed that she wondered if she ought to ask him in. But she was still a little cautious.

'They went on the morning train, to catch the afternoon flight – I'm not sure of the time of it, exactly –'

'I brought her straight here,' he said. 'Soon as I got this address, I brought her straight. I should have rung up. If only I'd rung up.' He was scratching his head in frantic distress.

'Brought *who* straight here?' asked Aunt Bee. She felt suddenly rather faint.

'His wife !'

When Aunt Bee revived, Bob explained. He insisted on explaining, even before Aunt Bee could rush out to the car to

137

see whether it really was her dear niece Meg, Rachel's mother, miraculously alive after all.

'It's her,' he said, and stood barring the door. 'I recognized her the moment I saw her. Convalescent Home in Holland. I'd come off a boat, and there am I walking along looking for a cup of coffee, and there she is over the other side of the hedge. They go in the grounds every day for exercise. Well you can imagine what I felt – anyway, to cut a long story short, she got picked up by a trawler; must have been in the sea longer even than we were.'

'But he said he saw her drown!'

'So did I. At least, the water went over her, and we never saw her again. Not that you could see anything, bar water. Or hear anything, either. It's a miracle anything could survive in that sea.'

'A miracle!' whispered Aunt Bee.

'Well, anyway, this Dutch Hospital took her in, she must have been in pretty poor shape, but they got her right enough to go to the Convalescent place, and –'

'But why didn't she write? or why didn't the hospital, the Police –'

'They couldn't,' he said. 'Nobody could do anything.'

'I don't understand.'

He took a deep breath.

'She's lost her memory,' he said.

Aunt Bee sat down with a flump on the hall chair.

'I called it a miracle!' she said. 'But it's a miracle with a sting in the tail.'

'That's why I didn't want you to see her until you knew,' he said. 'They say she may get it back, once she's back in some familiar place, people she knows. . . . But now they've gone.'

'But she knows me, she knows this place!' Aunt Bee rallied. 'Oh, let me see her, let me go to her!'

'There's a nurse in there with her. The Red Cross sent a nurse, in case I was wrong, see. But I'm not wrong. I'd have known her in a million. . . .'

But Aunt Bee was half way down the garden path.

An hour later, she was making tea again, with tears running down her round pink face. To think that Meg shouldn't recognize her. Meg, her favourite niece, who had climbed the apple tree as a little girl, and the pine tree later on, and then had brought Rachel, her own little girl . . .

Rachel. If only, if only they hadn't gone. Surely the sight of Rachel would have brought her memory back. Bob had rung up the Airport, in a last desperate hope – but no, the plane had left.

Never mind, said Aunt Bee to herself staunchly, and wiped away the tears. No use being sentimental. Never mind. They'll let me keep Meg here until I can get in touch with them . . . one has to take the long view. . . .

But it was difficult to take any view, at the moment, except that fate was ironical. The Red Cross nurse sat discreetly in the background and drank her tea; Bob looked miserable and spilt his in the saucer; Meg just looked pleasant, and healthy, and politely surprised. She obviously didn't know where she was at all.

The door knocker again.

'Esther must have forgotten her key, after all,' said Aunt Bee, and went to open it. She was almost relieved to escape for a moment from Meg's curious and yet unseeing gaze.

The faint shriek in the hall made Bob and the nurse jump up. Then another voice.

'It's him !' said Bob. 'I'd know that voice –'

He dashed out of the room, but not quickly enough. Rachel slipped past him, hurrying blank-faced into the warm. She looked, and stopped dead.

'A miracle, a miracle!' Aunt Bee squeaked in the hall.

Rachel's mother glanced up vaguely, and regarded Rachel with mild interest. Nothing else.

'. . . I don't understand,' her father was saying outside. 'What *is* all this? We had to come back, we missed the flight, the trains are all at a standstill – ice on the line.'

The words were flat and casual; he sounded very tired.

But Meg had become rigid. An extraordinary change transformed her face; particularly her eyes.

'*Rachel*!' she said.

'I never wanted to go to Australia,' said Rachel later, when they were all trying to calm themselves down with tea and hot toast. 'I don't even like kangaroos, much!'

'Never mind . . .' began Aunt Bee.

But then another voice broke in. From the front door, where it had let itself in, unheard.

'Bee, are you there? What's that car doing outside? My dear, I've had a dreadful time, quite dreadful . . . and I never even got to the Sales! It's a miracle I'm back at all. Ice on the line, my dear. Complete chaos. As I say, it's a miracle I ever . . .'

Then she came in and saw them all. It took three pieces of buttered toast and all the rest of the little jar of Marmite to persuade her that she was not dreaming.

EGLANTYNE JEBB

FOUNDER OF THE
SAVE THE CHILDREN FUND

AT the end of the First World War millions of children were dying from hunger and sickness and there was no one to help them. Eglantyne Jebb read about these children and was determined to do something about them. 'We must start a Save the Children Fund,' she told her friends, and because of her courage and enthusiasm The Save the Children Fund came into being. Its first committee a handful of friends; its first contribution, a half-crown from the apron pocket of her own house-keeper.

Eglantyne Jebb was born in 1876, when life was very different from today. There was no television or radio; no jets; no rockets or space ships. People did not travel much and had to make their own amusements at home. She had four sisters and a brother and lived in a big house in Shropshire. Her parents were quite rich and the children were educated at home by a governess. Eglantyne Jebb went to Oxford University and later became a teacher. She was always interested in the welfare of poor children, but not until the war did she realize what she really wanted to do.

By the time the war was over Eglantyne had realized that it was not enough just to send money and food to children in need. Skilled doctors, nurses and administrators were needed to use the money wisely and to teach people how to care for their children. So The Save the Children Fund grew into the great organization it is today, caring for thousands of children in more than twenty eight countries all over the world.

Eglantyne Jebb was never satisfied that the Fund was doing all it could for children and she spent months travelling in countries overseas. There were none of the comforts we have today and she often travelled long journeys by train or boat carrying no luggage but a small rucksack. She talked to kings and statesmen, to leaders of churches, including the Pope, and to ordinary people, persuading them to help her to help the children. She was determined not only to organize relief for suffering children, but to make people realize that it is everybody's business to protect children from need.

In 1924 she drew up a Charter of Children's Rights, and took it, herself, to Geneva, where it was adopted at once as the League of Nations' own Charter for Children. She died there in 1928 but the work she started still goes on wherever there are children in need.

Her Charter stated simply that:

Every child matters, whatever his country, colour or creed.

No child can be allowed to be hungry, sick or physically handicapped without someone going to their help.

The orphaned and abandoned child must be taken in and cared for.

The child must have a chance to work, to play and to learn so that he can grow up to be happy and useful.

All children should have a chance in life and if any of the world's children are able to learn and make use of their talents, they should use them for their own happiness and to help others.

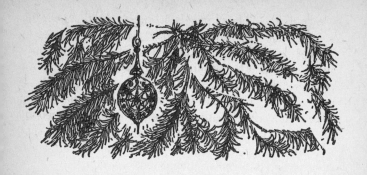

URSULA MORAY WILLIAMS

Terry's Tree

A FEW weeks before Christmas our kid brother said he didn't believe Christmas trees grew anywhere but in Woolworth's, and of course we all laughed at him.

Our kid is only four, and he's a spastic, but as bright as a button inside his head, and they are doing wonders for him at the Clinic, only it is slow, him being so small.

My mates all make a fuss of Terry, and they had taken to dropping in to have a word with him before we went out in the evening. Mick, who is two–three years older than the rest of us, seems even more crazy about Terry than we are, and when Terry said that, Mick said:

'What? You don't believe that, do you?' and Terry says: 'Yes.'

Mick said: 'Well, look at that now! and I know a wood where there are dozens of 'em growing, getting ready for Christmas, up on Mr Bosworth's place. We'll take him there Saturday, shall we boys? Like to come and see real Christmas trees growing, Terry?'

Of course he'd like to come! He talked of nothing else all the week, and Mick had a car so it was easy. Mick worked in a garage for Mr Garrod, who let him keep his car in the yard. Mick taught all us boys to drive in the yard and up and down the lane at the back that wasn't a public road but a kind of place belonging to Mr Garrod. It wasn't the first time Terry had been in Mick's car either, because he often came down to Garrod's on a Saturday along with us, and rode around in the back seat as happy as a king. He thought the world of Mick, who gave him nuts and bolts to hold in his bad hands, and it had kind of helped him with the exercises they'd taught him to do at the Clinic.

On Saturday we raced him down to Garrod's in his chair just as Mick came off work, with our Mum shouting after us to take care of Terry just as she always does.

We got in the car, pushchair and all, because Mick said Mr Bosworth didn't like cars on his private land and so we'd have to walk a bit, and anyway nobody was supposed to know the trees were there because of people stealing them for Christmas.

'How did you know they was there, then?' Chris asked.

'The boss and I was out there on a job,' said Mick, 'and I heard Mr Bosworth talking about it. But we don't have to go near his place to see them, anyway. We can get round the back and leave the car in the lane.'

That was just what we did.

Any of us boys would have carried Terry but he wouldn't even let Mick. He's got like that lately. He likes to feel he's too big to be carried outside the house. As if any of us couldn't pick up three like him without knowing it! But there it was, he sat up all proud in his chair as we pushed him up the lane and through a field, though you'd have thought it would shake the life out of him the going was so rough.

Mick didn't know quite where the trees were, after all, and

144

we'd walked quite a way when we saw them … a kind of plantation huddled up against the side of a wood … there must have been nearly a hundred of them. Nice little trees they were, none of them more than six feet tall, and some much smaller.

Terry just stared and stared.

'Nice, aren't they?' said Mick, crouching down beside him, 'I guess there's a hundred of 'em there. Now you don't believe they grow in Woolworth's, do you?'

'They aren't silver!' said Terry.

'Look at that now!' says Mick, pretending to be fed up with him. 'We bring him all this way and kill ourselves dragging him over the plough and he says they aren't silver!'

'I want one!' says Terry next.

'You want a tree and it's five weeks away from Christmas?' says Mick. 'You're too early, boy-o! You'll just have to wait, that's all!'

'Can I have one for Christmas?' Terry asked.

'Oh you'll have one for Christmas all right!' we all promised him.

'Which one?' Terry asked, just like a kid does.

'Which one do you want?' says Mick, as he puts his long legs over the fence and gets in among the trees. 'This one? This one?'

'Yes, that one!' says Terry, when Mick had touched four or five trees. He's clever, our kid, he had chosen the pick of the front row. It was a real smart little tree.

'That's it then!' says Mick, coming back.

'Why can't I have it now?' said Terry, keeping on.

'Why it isn't big enough yet!' Mick tells him. 'It's got to grow a bit more first. We'll leave it here to go on getting bigger for Christmas,' and he whisks Terry's chair around and had him across the field in a minute before the kid can make any fuss, not that he's like some kids, always whining and yelling, our Terry never does that, he's ever so easy and good.

Well after that there wasn't a day that he didn't talk about his tree. I should think the whole neighbourhood knew that he was going to have one and Mick was going to get it for him. We didn't let on where we'd been, and Mr Bosworth's place was quite a way off, so nobody was to know that there wasn't half a dozen plantations in between us and where the Christmas trees were growing.

It got to be quite a thing, getting ready for Terry's tree. We found a pot for him to put it in, and our Sandra brought him something pretty to hang on it almost every time she came home from work. Terry kept them in a box beside his bed. He was ever so proud of them.

Next Saturday he wanted to go and look at the trees again. He said he wanted to see if they had grown any bigger.

Well we were all going to see the League match so we couldn't take him and Terry cried a bit. Mick didn't like that and he said we'd take him the next Saturday for sure, so Terry cheered up.

We did go the next Saturday and Terry wanted to take one of his ornament things to hang on the tree he had chosen, to show it was his. 'Else I shan't know!' he said.

'All right, you do that!' says Mick, and Terry chose a smashing glass bauble, all silver with a red and blue flower on it. He couldn't hold it himself so we took it for him in case it should get broken.

I don't know how we got the chair there without tipping Terry out or the wheels coming off, but we did, and he was so pleased to see his tree again that he didn't worry over much about its not having grown an awful lot in the two weeks.

Chris had a bit of string and he tied the glass ball to the

Christmas tree. It looked ever so pretty. Then he gave a kind of a wink at Mick and I think they decided there and then that Terry was going to have that tree.

Anyway when Terry went on again about wanting to take it home with him Mick said, quite decidedly:

'We got to leave it just one more week, boy-o! and then next Saturday we'll come along with a spade and we'll dig it up for you!'

Later I heard Bob ask him if he thought he could square it up with Mr Bosworth through Mr Garrod, because all the boys would like to chip in and get it for Terry, and Mick said he thought he could do that all right.

So we arranged we'd be there the same time next week, and Mick would drive us out. This time as well as the lot of us and the pushchair we'd have to get the Christmas tree into the car, but I don't think anyone thought of staying behind. None of us wanted to miss the minute when Terry got his own tree and took it home.

He didn't talk so much about it all that week, but he kind of *lived* it, and his eyes were always on that box of ornaments. Sandra brought in some pieces of wire tied on a card, and showed him how you made hooks with them to hang the things on the tree, and Terry just grinned all over as if he couldn't wait.

Well we never thought about Saturday being bad weather, but it was. Bitter cold and dark and grey with nasty dashes of sleet and a wind that took the skin off you. Of course our Mum didn't want Terry to come out and Sandra joined in, and when the other chaps arrived we were all going at it hammer and tongs with Terry looking as if the end of the world had come.

Mick wasn't there, because we were going to meet him down at Garrod's, but Bob and Chris and Steve and Ken arrived, and the women began to pipe down a bit when they saw them all come in.

I said: 'He isn't made of sugar, Mum, and we'll be back in the house by four o'clock. I swear we will.'

Mum said: 'You'll be back in the house all right but no need to take him along too,' and I said: 'And him counting every minute of the week to go and dig his very own Christmas tree? Why, he's so full of it he won't even notice the cold !'

Mum said, relenting: 'Well it won't have to be a minute after four. Not one minute, David ! and he'll have to put on another coat on top of that one.'

So she and Sandra packed up the kid like he was a Christmas parcel sealed and registered for foreign parts, and we took him off joking and pulling his leg about what we should write on the label. But when we got down to Garrod's Mick wasn't there.

There wasn't anybody at the garage at all, and the pick-up van was gone that Mr Garrod used for going off on jobs, and

Mick used it too. We guessed they'd gone off now, or Mick had, and there was nothing to do but wait.

It was perishing cold, so some of the boys took Terry across to put him inside Mick's car that was standing in the yard like it always did. They gave a shout, and when the rest of us went over they'd found a note. There was a spade inside the car too.

Mick had written on the paper: 'Gone on job to Kinston with the boss. Back 3.30. M I C K.'

'That's torn it!' I said. 'Better take our Terry home. We can't wait about till half past three in this cold. And we can't get there and back in half an hour neither. More like two hours.'

Terry looked that miserable we couldn't bear to look at him, and we were all as cold as could be.

'Go on,' said Chris, 'I'll drive you! I'll be seventeen in January!'

We all knew he could drive all right, but there was the licence.

'You ain't got a licence, have you?' Ken said, rather weak-like. 'You'll get copped.'

'Oh I know a track through all the back lanes and across the common,' Chris says, already in the driver's seat. 'We won't go within miles of a copper. Put him in the back and hop on! Mick would be all for it. He wouldn't want the kid hanging about and getting cold.'

The way our Terry had cheered up was something wonderful. And he couldn't take his eyes off that spade.

'When you've dug it up you put it on my chair and I'll take it home!' he said, so that put paid to any idea about leaving the chair behind. We all piled inside and Chris started up the car, and shot out of the yard like Jack Brabham. He was right about the back lanes, he knew the way all right, and we hardly met another car, much less a copper.

It didn't seem so far across the fields from the lane as it had before, and two of us took charge of the chair and lifted it over the worse places.

So we got to the last field in no time at all, and walked along beside the coppice full of pine trees that hid the plantation of Christmas trees from the road.

It hid it from us too, so it knocked the lot of us for six when we turned the corner and saw that every Christmas tree was gone !

Cut down, they were, every single one of them ... just a lot of little stumps sticking out of the ground, and a wide empty space going on until it hit the willow copse on the far side.

I looked at the others and then I looked at our Terry, and he was perfectly white like when our Sandra let him fall down the stairs, and the other boys looked pretty queer too. Steve put down the spade with such a clang I thought he'd dropped it, but Terry didn't even blink.

'He's cut 'em !' Chris said, and he called Mr Bosworth names I don't say myself in front of the kid. 'I might have known it !' he said, 'they've been selling trees in town all the week.'

'We'll get you one in town, Terry !' Bob said to comfort him. 'We'll go straight back and buy one out of the shops !'

'A silver one from Woolworth's !' said Steve.

That didn't do nothing for Terry. He began to cry, ever so quietly, and he cried and cried. I know he was thinking there wouldn't ever be another tree like his own tree, and they'd taken it away with his silver ball on it. Well the little chap would feel it, naturally, and there wasn't anything much that we could do about it.

We were all trying to cheer him up and not thinking of anything else very much. So we never saw two men come walking out of the coppice until they were right on top of us.

They could only be the owner of the plantation, Mr Bosworth, and a police officer, and the next moment we were for
it.

'Is that your car in the lane?' the copper wanted to know,
and we said yes. Terry just went on crying. 'What are you
doing here?' was the next, and none of us could think of
nothing to say to that. We couldn't hardly say we'd come to
look at the Christmas trees when there weren't supposed to
be no Christmas trees to look at.

But we did say it after the next question, which was did
we know we were on private land, and we explained we'd
brought the kid to see the trees because he'd never seen
a Christmas tree growing before, so then they looked at
Terry.

'What's he crying for?' asked the man who was with the
policeman. 'Is he cold?'

'He's crying because the trees are gone !' Chris said.

'So you knew there was supposed to be trees there?' the
copper says, all suspicious.

We didn't say yes or no to that one.

'Is that your car in the lane?' he asks again.

We said yes it was.

'Is there any more of you here?' says the copper.

We said no there wasn't.

'Which of you is the driver?' snaps the copper.

Chris says he is. Funny thing, but Chris is older than most
of us yet he looks about twelve.

'You got a licence? I'd like to see it !' says the copper.

'I haven't got a licence !' Chris says.

'Oh you haven't, haven't you?' says the officer. 'Any of
you got licences? Any of you seventeen yet? Any of you
own that car?'

Well we had to say no each time, and our Terry just goes
on crying ever so quiet and miserable, not looking at the

copper or anyone, but staring at the place where the Christmas trees ought to be and wasn't.

'I'd like to ask these young fellers a few questions down at the station, Mr Bosworth, and if it's all the same to you I'll leave you for a short while,' the copper says when he has taken our names and addresses. 'I may get some light thrown on this tree-stealing business. I'll run 'em down in their own car and get hold of their parents....'

'If you think we've got anything to do with the trees being gone you're wrong about it,' Chris says. ''Cos we never had nothing to do with it. We've been out here a couple of times to show 'em to the kid, and we'd sort of promised him one, see? Mick O'Brien said he'd speak to Mr Garrod and try to fix up that we could collect one today.'

Mr Bosworth's face cleared when Chris said that.

'That's right!' he nodded, 'Jim Garrod told me last Thursday. Well that would have been all right, but somebody's got too big a mouth round here I guess. When I came along this morning the whole lot had been lifted.'

'It's hard luck on the kid!' Chris said after a pause.

Mr Bosworth and the policeman looked at Terry who was crying like his heart would break, and he doesn't look much at any time.

'Cheer up, son!' says Mr Bosworth kindly. 'The policeman only wants to ask your brothers a few questions. He isn't going to lock them up!'

'Our Terry likes policemen!' I said, a bit sharp I suppose, but the copper goes over to Terry and kneels down on the grass beside him.

'What's the matter old son?' he says, ever so friendly, and Terry talks at once, because as I say he's used to meeting coppers on the street, and he likes them, poor little kid.

'They cut down my tree!' he says, and he can't put his

hands in his eyes or wipe his nose so he looks a fair treat, 'And it's got my ball on it!'

We told the copper what had happened and he looked real upset. Mr Bosworth did too.

'If I could get my hands on the lot that took 'em!' he said. We got the message then that they didn't match us up with stealing the trees any more. Just as well seeing as there was the borrowed car to answer for, and having no licence or insurance, and driving under age.

'There's lots of trees in town. You tell your Dad what's happened! Father Christmas will get you another tree!' the copper says, and he takes out his hanky and wipes Terry's nose ever so nice. It got me perhaps he had kids of his own. Funny to think of a copper having kids.

'It ain't got my silver ball on it!' said Terry, and he didn't look like stopping crying this side of Christmas. 'The boys said it was growing bigger all the time, but it ain't there any more!'

And that time I'll swear I saw an idea arrive in the copper's head, right through the middle of his helmet.

'Growing, was it?' he said, and he got off the ground and stood up ever so big beside Terry. 'Getting bigger all the time? and with silver balls on it? Why son! I guess I know what they've done with your Christmas tree!'

He had to say it twice, because you know what kids are when they're bawling . . . they don't think of nothing but the thing that matters, and the next time he said it he didn't sound nearly so confident about what he was saying, but you should have seen Terry's face! He stopped crying all of a sudden and he looked and looked, as if the copper was going to bring his tree right out of a hat.

'Where is it?' he whispered, and the copper swelled up like a prize fighter in the ring. Then he leaned right over Terry and he said:

153

'Why! The Mayor sent for it! Best tree in the wood, he said, didn't he Mr Bosworth? get me the best tree, he says, if you have to bring the perishing lot to do it, he says, because I want to set it up outside the Town Hall for all the town to see . . . and there it is now!'

'It isn't!' said Terry, but the copper wasn't worried, and I guessed he *had* got kids of his own. He took hold of Terry's chair and switched him round in a flash. 'You come and see!' he says, setting off down the side of the wood at a good pace. 'And you come along too, you lot!' he calls to us over his shoulder, so we all followed him back to the car, and he gets into the driver's seat leaving Chris looking glum, and drives us back to town.

We didn't go down the back lanes this time. We went by the main road, past the Infant School, past the bus station, and the Grand Hotel, and into the High Street.

Terry was very quiet, sitting on my knee and just looking ahead. I didn't know if he'd taken in what the policeman had said or not, and I wasn't thinking about him much by then. I was wondering what my Dad was going to say to me, and what Mick would say for that matter. Everything had gone back on us and it did seem a shame that it should hit Terry too.

So I think I was just as surprised as he was when the officer swished the car round the corner by the Municipal Offices, and there, standing in the middle of the square, all lit up like a pantomime was the biggest Christmas tree I'd ever seen in my life, shining and sparkling although it wasn't anything like dark yet, and you should have seen our kid's face!

The copper was looking at him as happy as a prize tom cat.

'Grown quite a lot, hasn't it?' he said, as if he'd done it all himself, just for Terry. We were hard up against the tree now, on the kerb, and seeing a policeman in the car people had kind of drifted aside so Terry could see all he wanted to.

He just stared with all his eyes for a bit, and then suddenly something came into his face, and he jerked himself, and I knew he was trying to get his arm up and point. And I knew what he was trying to point at too, because I saw it at the same time as he did, hanging on a low branch of the Christmas tree, not so far from Terry's nose.

He said: 'That's my silver ball!' and there it was ... just like his anyway. Good old Woolworth's!

Well, Chris and the boys cheered, and some people began to sing Christmas carols, and the copper went on grinning and Terry looking and looking as if he'd never stop. And the copper said, quite low:

'Seeing as how you've all been straight about it, and if I check up that you really drove across the common and didn't pass our man on point near the traffic lights ... and if you all live at the addresses you said you did, then I shall have a word with your fathers, and maybe that's all you'll hear about it this time. I'm not promising, mind you ...'

But he kept his word.

Mick wouldn't speak to us for three days. He'd come back and found the car gone and he was hopping mad with the lot of us. We'd left the spade in Mr Bosworth's plantation too, and that was another nail in our coffins. We got into trouble at home, of course. Our Dad let it go with a ticking off, but Mum and Sandra never stopped screaming about it ... how they'd never have let Terry go, with Chris driving without a licence and uninsured. As if the kid would be worse hurt in an accident with an insurance certificate or without one! But I saw their point.

As for Terry, all that side of it passed him by. He just lived those days for the evenings when one of us would push him down to the Town Hall to look at his Christmas tree. We didn't hear if the real one ever got found or not. This was the real one for Terry. By the end of a fortnight we were sick of the sight of it, all except Terry. We were glad when they took it down ... and then he wanted his silver ball back! and of course the students who were taking the tree to pieces just routed about until they found it and gave it to him.

And after all, who wouldn't?

THE SAVE THE CHILDREN FUND
SPONSORSHIP SCHEME

LITTLE M'Hand is about seven years old. He was probably born in a village in the south of Morocco but nobody really knows. Neither is anybody sure whether little M'Hand has still got a mother and father. He himself does not know, but it is hard for M'Hand to be certain about anything because he is blind.

He was found wandering, and the village chief sent him to the Home for Blind Children in Taroudant which is run by The Save the Children Fund. Here he will be fed, cared for and taught to read in Braille. Later on, he will learn skills and handicrafts. But this bewildered little boy needs more than this. He needs a substitute for the family he lost. He needs to know that there is someone who really cares about him as a *person* so that as he grows up he does not have to cope with another handicap – loneliness.

The Save the Children Fund gives regular help with educational facilities, in health, and the provision of food. It also assists in increasing food production off the land. But it is an enormous task to meet all the children's needs adequately; even providing them with three meals a day presents quite a problem. There is just not enough money, or energy, for the things which will give them joy, so the Sponsorship Scheme was started. With its help it is now possible for people who care enough to 'adopt' an individual child, like M'Hand, or a family or group. The children and the sponsors are encouraged to write to each other, exchange photographs and tell one another about their lives, their families, hobbies, and all the other tit-bits that letters between friends contain.

Today there are more than 7,000 sponsored children getting this kind of personal attention in over 20 different countries, including Austria, France, Greece, India, Italy, Korea, Lebanon, Lesotho, Morocco, Malawi, Malta, Pakistan, Seychelles, Swaziland, Uganda, West Indies and Yugoslavia. The Scheme also helps about 300 British children. Recently the Fund has been seeking sponsorship for groups of children rather than individuals.

Altogether about 900 family group sponsorships are now being operated in Hong Kong, Korea, Greece, Uganda, Malawi, Morocco and the West Indies.

The Fund's Homes are usually divided into houses each of which has between four to seven rooms, and each room can be sponsored at the normal group sponsorship fee. Each room has an older boy or girl in charge, whose name is given to the sponsor. A group photograph is taken, and the boys and girls take it in turns to write to their sponsor.

The Save the Children Fund in London acts as a sort of clearing house for sponsorships. Its administrators in overseas countries send case histories of children they think will benefit from sponsorship, to the Fund's headquarters. Sometimes people choose each other because they have the same birth date, or the same name. One teenage English girl, who raised the sponsorship subscription on a special 'walk', chose to 'adopt' a ten-year-old boy who lives in the West Indies and who cannot walk because he is crippled. Children in overseas countries often have unusual names which attract sponsors – names like Pansy Cupid, Polycarp Dlamini, Let Us Pray, Happiness and Welcome.

A British judo club sponsors a boy in Korea, and a Regiment of the British Army takes a special interest in two eleven-year-old boys in Pakistan because the Regiment has been associated with Pakistan in the past.

Many famous people, too, have joined the scheme. Writers Noel Streatfeild and Elizabeth Goudge, Dame Flora Robson, the actress, and Benjamin Britten, the composer, have over the years done a great deal to help The Save the Children Fund.

It often happens too, that people who have been helped by SCF sponsors as children themselves 'adopt' a needy child when they grow up. Here is a letter which arrived addressed to the Sponsorships Organiser:

'As a child I was "adopted" by a Women's Institute in New Zealand. I think it was an Aunt Mona McAuliff, of Little River, Long Island. This was arranged through The Save the Children Fund as my mother became a widow when my brother and I were under school age. I know that my mother was helped a great deal by the gifts of soap, biscuits, and tinned food, and was very grateful.' She goes on to ask, 'I wondered if perhaps you could help me to help someone in the same way.'

A sponsored child apparently never forgets the help he has received. For this reason, no less than any other, the Scheme justifies its existence.

If you or the school you go to would like to help some child or group of children by joining the Sponsorship Scheme, please write for details to:

The Sponsorships Organiser
The Save the Children Fund
29 Queen Anne's Gate
London SW1

The costs are approximately £30 per year for an individual child, and £50 for a family or group, payable yearly or half yearly.